NO DIRECTIONS

Available simultaneously with this novel
Boy
An End and a Beginning

NO DIRECTIONS

JAMES HANLEY

With an introduction

by

HENRY MILLER

ANDRE DEUTSCH

All rights reserved.
First published in Uniform Edition 1946
by Nicholson & Watson 26 Manchester
*Square, London W.*1.

First published	*April* 1943
Second Impression	*April* 1943
Third Impression	*May* 1943
Uniform Edition	1946

First published 1943 by Nicholson & Watson

This edition first published 1990 by
André Deutsch Limited
105-106 Great Russell Street London WC1B 3LJ

Copyright © 1990 by the Estate of James Hanley

ISBN 0 233 98588 3

Printed and bound in Great Britain by
WBC, Bristol and Maesteg

INTRODUCTION

I woke up this morning thinking of *No Directions* and I let out a roar. I was thinking of Mr. Johns, the drunken sailor man, and of Clem, the little genius, and of Lena, his wife, suffering from "cancer of the heart." And I roared again. The book is one long roar of oceanic trash drowned in a green jungle of cracked ice, dementia, hysteria, vomit, flames and hallucination. It goes in every direction at once, with Mr. Johns the sailor man doing a tangential slide into limbo. Clem, the "geeney-wenius," is always putting a last touch to his immortal canvas; his wife is always looking for the pills or the vinegar rag; Mr. Johns is always looking for a bloody drink; the man with the Philco is always trying to get Bolivia; Gwen is always looking for her Richard, who in turn is always looking for dead bodies, incendiary bombs or a brief let-up in the ceaseless strafing from above.

Everything happens in a house in London during an air raid. It is a mad-house, an exact replica of the outer mad-house which is the world, only this mad-house is in the mind, and only a cataclysm can put an end to the crazy clock-work. The style which Hanley employs to register this fantastic *dégringolade* is superbly suited to his needs. One feels that the author is not merely in the seemingly meaningless suite of events which are piled on one another pell-mell but in the débris and bric-à-brac of the mind itself. It is the language of utter disorder and demoralisation, maintained as rigidly and consistently through-out as is Kafka's in the nightmare he inhabits. The humour is savage and explosive, maudlin and cracked by turns. It is high humour, the humour of the gods rolling in their cups. Not a single commentary, not even an oblique one, does the narrator permit himself. His is "the Arctic touch"—and it leaves a cold shiver down the spine.

v

One of the memorable scenes is that of the genius —
magnificently obsessed—moving his canvas back and forth, up
and down, in and out, from his miserable lodging upstairs to
the shelter down below. Hanley has made of this episode an
addition to the mythological images of ancient times. Clem
symbolises the modern artist moving in a void under the
pressure of his own steam. It is he who invents the "cancer
of the heart." And why not cancer of the heart? Isn't everything topsy turvy ? Why should the heart remain invulnerable ?
   At the height of the air raid the scene becomes apocalyptic.
"I must see this, I must see this !" cries Clem, and he tears
himself loose and steps out into the river of light flowing past.
Mr. Johns, the drunken sailor man who has been lying prostrate
on the floor of the shelter, is now lying outside, blown outdoors
by a violent concussion. Clem looks at him for a moment or
two, then he steps over "his great shuddering arse." The
description of what follows is like a passage out of Revelation.
One is blown along like dust, lifted and whirled aloft like a
blazing cinder. Consuming everything is the vast ocean of light
in cataracts of blazing, drenching colours. "God !" he said,
"it's magnificent, it's——." Clem scrambles about, intoxi-
cated you might say, by the stupendous destruction. He is on a
roof looking down. "Far below in the street a grinding of
brakes, hissing noises, but always the light overhead, reeling,
bright colours, like an overflow from revelries. . . . Wood and
stone and steel alive with wrecking power. . . . An orgy of
movement, in one direction, moving under the light. An ocean
of floating trash." Suddenly he walks off the roof ! Now he is
wrestling with a mad white stallion, he is being dragged along,
he feels himself become one "with all this rushing ocean."
The stallion has begun to gallop but he holds on grimly—"as
though all his life had been a single movement towards this,
to hold fast with a hoofed creature, demented in a rocking
city." Finally he quiets the animal's fear, it calms down, and
together they walk slowly down the shattered street. "If you
walked far enough you came to something green, older than
steel or stone, where this beast belonged."
   The drunken sailor meanwhile has passed into the final

stupor of oblivion. He had been trying to get to Plaistow all through the book but succeeds only in wandering from one room to another and at last winds up in the deathless sea of light where delirium tremens continues forever. Lena the wife is waiting for Clem to return, then they will climb back to their hollow shell, to the pain in the chest and the pills. Clem, having left the horse in a field, does return, sees the sailor's prone figure again, mumbles "Nothing," then asks Lena if she is ready. "I'm ready now," she says, and the blankness of the page indicates to us that we may now begin all over again, get the canvas hoisted to the top floor, put the vinegar compress around poor Clem's aching head, wander into the green room, take a swig from some absentee's liquor bottle, search for the right depth and the right colour, turn the Philco on and off, get Bolivia at all costs, laugh again, make love with the inebriated model on the table, on the floor, or from the chandelier if capable, then switch out the lights, drag the canvas down the dark stairs again, walk over the roof tops, dive into the churning light, die on the pavement of a shattered street in an ocean of trash, and thus, little by little, step by step, up and down, backwards and forwards, inside and out, reeling, swooning, vomiting, chortling, try, as Mr. Eliot would say, "to grasp the essential horror of it all."

HENRY MILLER.

CHAPTER I

AFTER the deluge of sound ceased, after the wind passed, the sailor fell, was sick. They were in a desert of air.

"Goddam ! Get me out of this," the sailor shouted.

"Stand up," the little man said ; he began to pull. Crunching sounds came up.

"It's ice," the sailor said. "Get me out of this." Falling again, hands became feelers, pawed about. "I know ice," he said, "always something moving under ice, I know."

"Glass, you crazy bastard," the little man said, the cheap raincoat dripped water, his tin helmet kept falling over his forehead. "Stand up !" Half-bent, arms encircling the sailor, he pulled, pulled hard.

"Damn and blast you," he shouted, "why, you're drunk."

The moon came from behind a sheaf of slow-moving cloud. The sailor sprawled, the little man stood erect, his neck felt cold against the wet collar of his coat. He was watching a black shape, it seemed to be pushing itself up and up, to toppling height, but the moon passed behind cloud, they were in darkness again. He bent down, started to pull.

"Leave me alone," the sailor said.

"I dunno what the hell you want," the little man said. "First you ask me to get you out of this, shaking like a bloomin' jelly you were, and now you say leave you alone. Wish I could. You could stand about on the bloody ice all night then, if you liked. But that's just what I can't do. Come on ! Get up ! Being alone don't count any more,

9

nobody can be alone any more, see ? Now get up. Don't know who the hell you are, where you come from, but you can't lie there. I'm going to get you in some place. See ! Now come on. Be a good chap, pull yourself together. We all lose our bearings at times, course we do. But I'm not going to stand over you all night. Now ! Up you come.''

He shouted, ''*Up, up*,'' heaving, feeling a little breathless, the helmet fell again, right over his eyes, he could feel its steel rim on his nose.

''Blast you,'' he said.

''It's ice, I tell you.''

''All *right* then,'' savagely, ''it's ice. You're on a whole, bloody shining sea of it. See ! There's a broken berg over there.''

Desperate, he kicked the sailor, then began to drag him over the sea of glass. He was moving towards a door, only a vague shape in his mind as yet, but he was moving towards it, he knew he would put this sailor behind it, he was filled with resolution, nothing else mattered but to get this fool behind a door. The man was drunk. Suddenly the sailor dragged himself to his feet.

''Get me out of this.''

''I'm getting you out. Half a mo ! I'll go behind you and push. Keep your feet.''

He began pushing from behind. ''I can assure you, chum, that this is not ice, this is no sea, there are no icebergs floating about, no rocks or reefs. You've had more than you should. But I wouldn't blame you, not me. You'll be all right after you've had a sleep.''

''Have a horror of ice,'' the sailor said, blubbered, ''time is it ?''

''Listen !''

A nearby clock was striking. They went on, the little man pushing hard, slithering and sliding, inwardly cursing the sailor, his hands pressed into the small of his back.

''Hell ! *Move*, will you ?'' The sailor's arms were out-spread, his overcoat flapped like a bellying sail, he was hatless, from time to time he lost himself in incoherent mumblings.

He dragged on, groped about, halted, went on again, shouted at the top of his voice, "Where the hell am I ?"

"Nearly there," the little man said, the big black door now clearer in his mind. If he put out a hand he knew he could touch the door.

"Get him behind this door and then he can do what the hell he likes. My responsibility's finished."

He smiled, thinking of a man standing in the middle of a roadway, arms waving, crying, "Ice."

"Tight ! Thought he was in the bloody Arctic, 'spect," laughed a little, thinking of the sailor's shout. "Goddam ! Get me out of this," thinking of this and of many people running, all gestures, not a word spoken until he heard that frantic shout, "Ice."

"Aye, drunk all right. · Getting drunk, that's a gesture, too."

He stopped suddenly, said, "Here we are." He couldn't see the door but he knew it was there. He said reassuringly, "You'll be all right now," then let go his hold on the sailor. He bent down, picked up a large sheet of glass, held it to the sailor's face, said, "*Now* ! Now you have to believe me."

He took a little torch from his pocket, shone it on the glass. "See ! Glass ! And not only that, but if you look closely at it you'll see its coloured, something like a head on it, too. Now how the hell can that be ice ?" laughing loudly. "You've been having a good time, that's what it is, mate. I don't blame you, anyhow. Come on."

He was pushing and pulling again. "You sleep it off, you'll be all right when the light comes. Here we are."

He shone the torch ahead. They were before this door. The man kicked and the door fell in. They walked in over it.

"Go on ! Hell, *do* go on, will you ?" shouting into the sailor's ear, who still dragged his way over ice-fields, saw glassy, transparent seas, watched bergs float by, heard great boulders falling.

"Only the door fallen in," the little man said, pushing the sailor with all his strength.

"There ! Now you see what I mean," a little breathless

"the door. A door. No keys required. Being alone don't count any more. My job's finished. You're in. Got a match?" and without waiting for the other's reply, pulled a box of matches from his pocket and pushed them into the sailor's hand. "Here! You'll find some place to sleep all right. Good night."

He was gone. The black door was propped up again. He went off. After a while his crunching steps died away. The sailor struck a match, it immediately went out. He struck another, it shook between big, clumsy fingers, it burned. "Hell!" he said, "oh, hell, where the devil am I?"

He struck another match, he was in a long dark corridor. High, green painted walls, exuding damp, showing a film of damp, much broken plaster, a tiny pattering sound, a draught. Rain came in through a hole in the wall. He bent down, put his hand on the floor, felt there. Striking a match again he saw faded, dirty linoleum, patches of white where a hall-stand had once stood. Looking behind him he saw the door propped up; looking up he saw a big flight of stairs. The match burned out and he struck another. There was somebody standing at the top of the stairs, staring down, hands gripping the stair-rails. The match flickered out.

"Aye, aye," the sailor shouted, quite involuntarily, belched, began laughing, tried to strike yet another match, but the box fell to the floor. He began groping for it, suddenly sprawled, lay there, threw his arms up, called out, "Aye, aye."

The man at the top of the stairs was coming down, slow, unsure, a long journey to him, he kept tight hold on the rails. Half-way down he stopped dead, called in a thin, cracked voice, "That you, Mr. Jones?" Waited for the answer, the hands gripping the rail seemed suddenly convulsed, making a quick tapping sound, he couldn't clutch, he called, "That you, Mr. Jones?" He began to descend again.

When he reached the bottom he walked slowly in the direction of the front door, kicked the sailor's box of matches, jumped at the sound, bent down and found the box. He took a match out and struck it, saw a man lying on his back, said sharply, nervously, "Who are you?"

"Aye, aye," the sailor said. "Hallo there," he said. "Bugger me," he said.

"Who *are* you ?" the old man said, holding another match above his head, staring at a tall thin man, flat on his back, long-faced, long-nosed, thinning hair, a big mouth half open, opening and closing eyes, like shutters, like blinds going up and down, on darkness, on a desert of air, on a sea of ice.

"I came in over the ice," the sailor said, stretching his legs, suddenly shouted, "Aye, aye there," broke wind, laughed, began to sing.

At the same time the black door fell in. The old man swung round. "That you, Mr. Jones ?"

"Yes, it's me."

"I'm glad, glad," moving slowly in the direction of the door.

"There ! That's done it," Mr. Jones said, heaving a sigh of relief. He turned round, shining his torch on the old man. Then he saw the man on the floor.

" Who's there ?" The torch shone downwards. "Looks like a sailor to me."

"You're *all* right, Mr. Jones ?" the old man said.

"Oh, I'm all right."

"Come and help me," the old man said, ignoring the man on the floor.

"*Sure* you're all right ?" nervously, anxiously.

"Hell, I'm all right, Mr. Frazer. You go on ahead. I'm behind you. Don't worry."

They reached the foot of the stairs.

"There's the quarter hour just striking now," Mr. Jones said quietly.

They began to ascend. Mr. Jones shone the torch on the sailor, exclaimed casually, "Deado," then went slowly up behind Mr. Frazer. "Careful," he said.

"These stairs are bloody shaky now," he said, "watch that fifth stair, big hole there."

Mr. Frazer did not answer him. They went up in silence, until quite suddenly a telephone bell started ringing, the sounds struck forth as into an abyss, a door on the first floor opened, notes from a piano floated out, the door shut again, somewhere a woman was coughing. The bell went on ringing.

"Careful, easy," Mr. Jones said, feeling a frenzy in the hands that clutched his coat. "Easy, Mr. Frazer."

"That bell, drives me mad, starts to ring, never stops," added quickly, excitedly, "the torch, shine your torch, Mr. Jones."

Below a door banged, the sounds reverberating round the house.

"Always ringing," Mr. Frazer said, "nobody ever answers it."

"Well, here we are at last," Mr. Jones said, putting a hand on the old man's shoulder. "Now, don't worry, you'll be all right."

"It's not me. It's her. Her all the time. Something happened to our room door—she——"

Laughing loudly Mr. Jones said, "Oh that, we all know about that," waving his left hand over his head, "right off the bloody hinges, too. We'll soon fix that. Here's your room."

He shone the torch upon a half-open door. He pushed the old man in. "Glad you're all right, Mr. Jones," Mr. Frazer said, "thank-you, thank-you," and with desperate suddenness, "but it's this, *this*, I didn't mean the front door, I meant this."

The torch was shining fully on his upturned face. He whispered fiercely, "it's her, not me. It's Emily."

"Emily," Mr. Jones said, half-laughing, "Emily," the upturned face, the terrified eyes under bushy brows, the thin form lost in the folds of a dirty dressing-gown, the trembling mouth, something funny, a joke. "Emily—who's Emily?"

Almost coldly Mr. Frazer said, "My wife. You know it is. You forgot."

"Hell, yes, blast, so much has happened, so much is happening, so quickly, breath-taking, can't remember everything. Well—— ?"

"It's her, Mr. Jones," a break in the old man's voice,

words tumbling out hastily, confused, mere mumbling, something about the door, Emily was frightened about the door. His hands gripped the knob, shook there, the knob was rattling nearly half a minute before Mr. Jones realized it, exclaimed loudly, "but what's the matter, *really* ? Afraid. Of what ? What's up with the door ?"

The torch was turned out, they leaned on each other.

"Last night," the old man said, "we were asleep. We heard terrible noises, I woke up. The door was like you see it now. Won't open, won't shut, it's getting on Emily's nerves——"

"But——"

And almost in anguish the other exclaimed, "Won't shut, look ! look !"

"Keep cool, Mr. Frazer, I'll fix it," Mr. Jones said, and began tugging at the door, which would not budge. "Damn !" he kicked it, then flung his whole weight upon it.

"No, no," Mr. Frazer said, "don't do that. The noise, she can't stand much more of it. If we could only get the door to shut. Can't sleep."

"Let's go in, anyhow," Mr. Jones said, "let's get in. You'll catch your death of cold, only that dressing-gown over you a night like this. Go on, Mr. Frazer, go in." He pushed, they were in the room.

"Switch the light on, Emily." The room was flooded with light.

The old woman sitting up in the bed said, "Thank goodness."

"This is Mr. Jones, dear."

"But we've already met, haven't we, Mr. Jones ?" Emily said ; she shook violently as she spoke.

"I've been telling him about the door, Emily," Mr. Frazer said. He turned to Mr. Jones, "Sit down—you don't mind ?" Watching Mr. Jones sit gingerly on a cane chair.

"*Me* ! Not at all," Mr. Jones said ; he threw back his tin hat and a riot of black curly hair shot free. "Mind if I smoke ?" lighting a cigarette in the same instant. He puffed away irritably, he was ill at ease. He wondered why. It seemed odd, then, looking at Emily he realized at once. It was Emily. Something about her, the way she looked at him, now, this very moment, as he sat on the chair, something that sent uneasiness over him like a wave, he wanted to laugh. It was funny feeling so disturbed by an old woman sitting up in bed. He said abruptly, "Excuse me, I must go, got a job to do," jumped to his feet, smiled at Emily, made for the door, Mr. Frazer trailing at his heels, and Emily suddenly shouting after them, " Oh, God ! Fix the door."

Mr. Jones said, " Good night," passed through into the corridor, the old man at his heels, clutching at his coat, "Please, please, Mr. Jones," blubbering, "*please*——"

"Now look here, Mr. Frazer. You're upset. I can see that. But we all are. A thoroughly bad evening, *bloody*," something was impelling him to say, "and that's not all," but the words remained lifeless on his tongue.

"You'll be all right," patting Mr. Frazer's shoulder. "Go back to bed, everything'll be all right."

He stood erect, looking towards Mr. Frazer's room. He felt the old man's hands clutching at the lapels of his coat. He gripped the torch in his hand, switched it on, looked down at the old man.

"It's not me, I tell you ; it's her. You don't understand," Mr. Frazer said.

"The sailor, is that what she's afraid of ?" Mr. Jones said.

"It's the door," Mr. Frazer said, "can't you do anything ?"

"To-morrow, perhaps," abrupt to the point of rudeness. "I'm bloody tired. All in. See you in the morning. Good night. Remember, don't worry about——"

"It's Emily," the old man said, "poor Emily," speaking into space, "the poor dear."

Mr. Jones heard the rattling of the knob as he climbed the next flight of stairs, he could see Mr. Frazer quite clear in his mind, saw him rattling at the knob, as though it held the very secret of the door's stubborness. Saw him pushing at it, pulling at it, hands finally falling to his sides, eyes staring helplessly at the door, and Emily's dry, shrill voice shouting, "Shut it, shut it."

"Poor Mr. Frazer," he said, "poor Emily," treading much plaster on the next landing, finally came to a door which opened as though by magic, and a smiling girl was standing there, welcoming arms out.

"Darling."

"Hallo dear," Mr. Jones said, embracing her. "You all right?" kissing her, "well, here I am back again."

"I've something nice and hot for supper," she said.

They went in. He closed the door, shut out sounds of a ringing bell, a singing sailor, a woman coughing on the ground floor.

He slumped into a chair, stretched his legs, threw his head back. He slept whilst she fussed about, setting the table, stirring something in a pan on the gas stove, peeping from behind the kitchen door, looking at him, the black face, the lines under the eyes, finally she came in and stood over him. He snored gently. She stroked his hair, sat on the arm of the chair, kept looking into his face, heard the kettle boil, got up and went out. She returned later with a tray.

"Wake up, darling," she said, "wake up. You can go to sleep again as soon as you've had your supper."

She put the tray on the table.

"Do wake up, darling."

"Oh, yes," he said, with shocked surprise, yawned, stretched himself, finally sat up.

She gave him tea, a plate of hot stew, some bread and butter. He began to eat, slowly, casually, he wasn't really very hungry, all the time looking directly at her, but he said nothing. A word now would have spoiled everything. Looking at her, there was something about just looking at her, noting the red and wavy hair, the oval pale face, her eyes, whose colour could not be defined, they might have been grey, a palish blue, but colour was never much to him ; he liked the clearness in them, like that of water. How calm her hands were, quietly folded in her lap. Suddenly he said, "You're not eating," and the spell was broken, her sudden smile was the ripple in the calm lake. That was the word. She was as calm as a lake.

"*Do* eat something."

"Yes, dear. All right. You *do* look so tired," she said. You'd better lie down. I won't talk, won't ask you silly questions, Richard. More tea ?"

She refilled his cup, put her own back on the table, came and sat on the arm of his chair, put an arm round him.

"God ! But I'm glad you're back, Dick," bending over him, kissing the back of his red and roughened neck, "you don't know——"

"I see he made a nice mess here," Richard said, "did you go down to the——"

"Yes," quickly interrupting him, "but I didn't stay there long, came back up here. I feel safer here. And I began to do things. Down there nothing seemed to have any meaning, but here——" and she was crying.

He put his cup down on the floor, took her in his arms. "Never mind, darling. Next week I'll have a different shift," and then his mouth was full of her hair ; he felt her whole body shiver to him, her sobs relieved him. If she had not cried he would have been afraid.

"Darling," he said, "darling" ; he wanted to cover her completely with this great, upthrusting tenderness that he felt. He held her tight. "Darling," he said.

Like children, they were suddenly, easily asleep.

The kettle left on the gas-jet spluttered, rattled its lid. The gas-fire in the small living-room drenched with its heat. Somewhere behind the wainscoting a mouse pattered about. Flies buzzed around the naked light bulb, the light glared down on them. The man snored, she seemed hardly breathing. The tropical birds on the wall-paper, perched and poised, seemed ready to burst into song, the background of deep foliage shimmered under the room's heat. It suggested Africa, the curve of the torrid zone. The man's snores were louder. Once the girl's body shook violently, the man said something in his sleep, murmuring into the dense mass of her hair. Above their heads feet endlessly paced the floor, the telephone bell went on ringing below stairs, but these two were secure, beyond staggering worlds, over a frontier in time.

" What's that ?'' she cried in dream.

It woke him. He sat up, shouted loudly, "What's the matter ?''

They were awake. His hand on her forehead felt sweat.

"Lord !'' he said, "the heat ! Phew !''

He freed himself, left her comfortable in the chair.

"All right, dear, go to sleep. Go to sleep again. Phew ! That blasted gas-fire.''

"The kettle, Richard, the kettle,'' its rattling sounds sinking fathoms in her mind.

"All right. I'll switch it off,'' he said, dashed into the kitchen, shut off the gas. The burned hole in the kettle disgusted him, he banged it down on the stove.

"What woke you ?'' she said, when he came back into the room.

"*That* !'' curtly, jerking a thumb in the door's direction, "*that*.''

"What, dear ?'

And in a sudden burst of anger he shouted, "Oh that ! Listen !''

She listened.

Somebody was talking outside the door. They were quite still, listening.

.   .   .   .

"I tell you again, he won't see you,'' a woman's voice said, tired, exasperated. "Why wait ?''

"But he knows me. I was astonished to hear he had begun work again.''

"He has never stopped working,'' the word sharp, direct, they struck air with the final ring of an ultimatum.

"Listen,'' Richard said.

"I am,'' the girl said.

"But why outside this room ?'' Richard said ; "it's that damned fool above. I wonder where the hell he aims to get to with all that walking, up, down, up, down. I wonder where he——''

"Ssh !" the girl said, "just listen."

"How many times have I to tell you that he won't see anybody." It was the older woman speaking, the one Richard knew, the one his wife, Gwen, knew.

"Not when he's working, won't see anybody," her voice rising, a sort of blind desperation behind it, "I tell you he won't——"

Richard flung open the door.

"Oh, hell, all *right*," he shouted, "all *right*. But can't you talk somewhere else ?"

He paused, then his tones were softer, "but not so loudly. People want to sleep. I've been out all day, and half the night. There's plenty of room down there," pointing towards the landing, the darkness, the void. He stood looking at the two women. Yes, he knew one all right, but the other. No, she was a complete stranger to him. He looked at her. Young as Gwen was, pretty as Gwen was, but not as calm. One look could tell him that, the face was disarmed, helpless under the bright, vicious light from his room. He looked from her to the older woman. A person of medium height, clasping a man's overcoat about her shoulders, a mass of grey hair drawn back from the forehead, so heightening a natural severity of expression, and in the pale, almost masculine features, two burning eyes. He looked at the long white hands clasping the overcoat. He said irritably, "Well ?"

The woman walked up to him. She watched him as she stroked back her hair, the overcoat fell loose, he saw a night-dress under it, he met her look.

"Have we disturbed you ? Have we ever given you one minute's trouble ? Has *he* ? Have we ever opened our mouths, even though we are surrounded by people whose mouths are never shut ? Do we talk ? Do we make gestures, do we throw up our arms, do we shout ?" the words came streaming out, feverish, tumbling off the tongue ; "what trouble have we ever given you ? I ask you that, Mr. Jones."

"Oh, I know," Richard was stammering back at her. I understand, I——"

And then his eyes caught sight of her mouth : he could not

take them off, he went on staring at it. "I mean, well—"
he was saying.

"Don't presume," she said. "*You* understand nothing."
The words came like a hiss from her piteous mouth.

He suddenly remembered he was tired, tired to the bone,
tired to the nerve's sharp edge. "Oh, God! Will you go
away?" he shouted in her face.

"Richard! Darling!" Gwen was at the door instantly,
her arm round his waist, looking at the two women, looking
beyond them, looking up at Richard, again at the two women,
as yet they were but shapes.

"Oh, do come in, Dick," she said; "you're tired out,"
and to the women, "Please, we don't mind you talking, but
don't talk so loudly, *please*."

The younger woman seemed to be hiding behind her
companion. But now she came slowly round and looked at
Richard.

"There's a bell ringing somewhere downstairs," she said;
"it's been ringing ever since I came in," suddenly started to
giggle, exclaimed, "Somebody's having a time of it."

"I tell you for the last time he won't see you. *I know.*
Never when he's working. Good night."

They watched her go, heard her climb the stairs.

"Was it something very important?" Gwen said.

"Not very. An old friend, that's all. Sorry to bother you.
Good night."

"Good night," Gwen said; suddenly realized she was
shivering, but she stood there watching the young woman
moving away towards the stairs. Richard went in, he pulled
her after him.

"Fancy jabbering away like that right outside people's
doors. As if it's not bad enough already, listening to him
pacing up and down," Richard said.

He was furious, but she met his anger with a smile. "You're
tired out, darling, do go to bed. Rest while you can, you
may be out again soon."

She crossed the room and switched off the gas-fire.

"The awful heat, and yet I'm shivering."

Richard said, "To-morrow I'll get the post office to come along and smash down that bloody ringing telephone; getting on my nerves.   Somebody else might oblige, but why talk of the devil."

They did not undress. Gwen put out the light. They talked in the darkness.

" The sheer rudeness of that woman in the overcoat," Gwen said.   "I never liked her, *never*."

"Don't bother yourself, darling.   It's nerves, I suppose. Nerves are ten a penny these days."

"All the time I was waiting for you to come in that piano was playing," Gwen said, stretching out on the divan, fingers roaming in Richard's hair.

" Wireless," he said. " I've heard it. Whoopee for somebody. It's that airman, home on a leave, I suppose. They know how to get drunk. Drink that sailor under the table, I'll bet, which reminds me, dear, have *we* anything left to drink ?"

"Gin.   Some rum, too, I think, darling."

"Good !   Let's have some.   What about rum ?   *Hot* !"

He was off the bed instantly, switching the light on, standing at the cupboard, bringing a bottle out.

"Hell !   That kettle," he said.   "Better get another kettle to-morrow, dear, this one's finished."

He went outside to heat some water in a pan. He put sugar in the drinks.

"Here you are, dear !   What'll it be—good health, a fine day to-morrow, or say just the skin off your nose ? that's the sailor's touch, that is."

"Yesterday's smile," Gwen said.

"Excellent," Richard said, raising his glass high.   "To yesterday's smile.   Don't know what it means of course, but it's new, isn't it ?" smiling.

They drank.   Gwen said, "You'll learn, it isn't new, dear," sipped her rum.   "I've just remembered.   Did Mr. Pasy call for that inventory, that list ?"

"The what ?"

"Oh! That list. You know the thing I made out this morning. It's wanted."

"Oh! It's on the sideboard there, I think. I never touched the thing."

He finished his drink, got the sheet of paper from behind a vase, returned to the divan, lay down, began to read aloud.

"Basement: Nappoo! Ground floor: Miss Benson, Miss Cleate. No. 1, out of town, Mr. and Mrs. Frazer. First floor, No. 2: Warden and Mrs." laughing, "No. 3, Mr. and Mrs. Robinson. Third floor: that's that airman chap. Mr. and Mrs. Clem Stevens. Fourth floor: No. 5, One, two, three—nine altogether. That's odd!" He paused, exclaimed very excitedly, "Heavens, there's an empty one here, too. Never thought of that."

"Put the light out, Richard, I'm tired."

"All right. And let's hope for a good night, shall we?"

He was staring up into the darkness long after she fell asleep.

"Six months ago I was peddling chemicals, vitamins, drugs—and now—those two silly bitches left no keys. Serve them right if something comes down and their stuff goes up," thinking of Miss Benson, Miss Cleate.

"Good heavens! That sailor chap," he exclaimed.

"Forgot all about him. Can't leave him down there."

He sat up, Gwen slept. He removed himself quietly from the bed, crossed the room in stockinged feet, bumped into the table, said, "Damn!" Then he opened the door and went out. He put the key in the lock, turned it noiselessly, and made for the stairs. He passed the room where the wireless screeched, light came in a splash from under the door. He went on, his mind was suddenly full of the sailor. He thought of him in terms of physical gestures, bound to a mast, open-mouthed before a furnace door, flat on his back in an open boat, a face after the torpedo's tear, all shock and smother. He knocked his toe, cursing. "Fancy forgetting him. Poor swine."

He came to the next flight of stairs, and then he saw somebody standing at a door, stopped dead, thought instantly,

"Oh, hell ! Those old fools and their bloody door."

He kept against the wall, there was no light on this landing, none on the next floor down. He would get past. Drawing nearer he saw, not a man, but a woman. It was Emily. She was standing in the doorway of her room. It was so quiet he could hear old Mr. Frazer snoring.

"Silly old fool. Standing there a night like this."

He overbalanced in his caution, veered away from the wall, clawed empty air, almost fell. She saw him. A figure, moving. He thought, "Oh, blast ! I'll be held up here. I don't mind *him*, he's half balmy anyhow. But her——"

He stood quite still. He wanted to laugh outright. There was something extraordinarily funny about to-night—he crept nearer. Would she see him ? He wondered, even as she said, softly, tremblingly, "It won't shut."

He thought, "Now what shall I say ? Oh, blast me for a fool. Hang the bloody sailor."

Their eyes met.

"God ! What shall I say ?" his mind groping for words.

Hardly realizing it, he was moving, passing her, saying nothing, she looking not at him, only somewhere beyond him, one bony hand gripping the door, the other listless at her side. Her face was a white blot in surrounding darkness. He was past her, safe, secure, past her who did not care much, her gesture grown from a word, a moment, a terror, seeing beyond him, out of darkness.

"Hell," Richard said, felt suddenly relieved, said again, "Hell !"

"I'll try to get their door fixed for them to-morrow. One realizes something. They are old. They are afraid."

He was going down the last flight of stairs. Cold draughts of air came up, struck at his face, a feeling of sheer emptiness, stair by stair descending, listening. The telephone bell had ceased to ring, the singing sailor was silent. No song. No snores. He was standing in the long hall, still listening. Silence.

"I say," he began, the words trembled out, others fluttered about in his mind like wild birds, like pigeons seeking home. "I say, there."

The echo came back to him as from a tremendous vault. He crept on, searching for some loose matches in his pocket, he struck one on the damp wall, the light blinked in damp air, he looked down. Nothing there. The sailor was gone. The black front door was up, but the sailor was gone. He wondered where, he wondered, for no reason at all beyond fugitive curiosity ; why ? Why had he gone ?

"Damn and blast him," Richard said loudly.

He felt defeated. Slowly he made his way upstairs again. Emily might still be there, one with the petrified wood, light would shine from under a door behind which an airman lived with his ecstatic smile, his laughter vats. With violently shaking hand he would endeavour to get Bolivia on his Philco set, yet nothing save music would float out. But now he could go up, pass these things, he wouldn't think of them, nor of that woman who kept her mouth shut, her body lost in the folds of an outrageous coat. Wouldn't think, and wouldn't be angry any more, something in his mind had cooled, something ceased its pecking, its scratching ; his mind was clean of these things. He returned as quietly as he came. He felt his way across the kitchen, touched the foot of the divan bed.

"Emily," he found himself saying half-aloud. "Reminds me of an actor I once saw standing in the wings, waiting." He struck the final match softly against his trousers, held it aloft. Gwen was fast asleep, Gwen was in dreamland.

"God ! I'm tired," Richard said, lay back, yawned, was soon snoring. The sudden riot of noise on the floor above did not wake them. Somebody was pushing a chair or bed across the floor.

.   .   .   .

The woman in the overcoat had pushed a big horse-hair sofa right to the other end of the room. She stood erect,

looked up and down, surveying, her chest hurt a bit, she
wondered if the effort was really worth while, she supposed
it was.

"There !" she said, "there now."

A long room with a high ceiling, a riot of canvases about,
the walls covered with them, a heap lying behind the grey
curtains, a heap against the wall by the door. Everything
was dusty, even the battered typewriter that stood on the
rickety card-table. They had lately moved in. An enormous
grate and a glimmer of fire within, at any moment it must
vanish, a distant smell of something frying. One great canvas
hung over the chimney-piece. Stood back from the fire was
another couch, it sprawled there, its leather rubbed a dirty
brown, a strip of carpet in front of it, shockingly bright.
And at the farthest end of this carpet a large black tom-cat.
At the right-hand side of the fireplace a cane armchair, in
which a man sat, a cigarette stump in his mouth, puffing
distractedly.

"Is that any better ?" she said. The figure in the chair
moved, he made to get up, suddenly sat down again.

"I suppose it'll do," he said, the cigarette bobbing up and
down as he spoke.

"*Do* say, be definite, will it do ?"

"Yes, dear ! That's fine," his voice a little weary. He
drew his chair nearer the fire. "No letters ?" spitting out
the cigarette, lighting another one.

"No letters ! Do you want your gruel ?"

"In a minute."

She took off her overcoat and went off to the other end of
the room, disappeared behind red curtains, after a moment
or two came out again, she wore her own dressing-gown.
She went to the card-table, looked at some letters and cards.
A circular about the spiritual values of water came out of a
long buff envelope without a sound. She looked at a card,
gilt-edged, beautifully white, she liked the clean look of this,
but it had a cold feel, a granite touch. She read an invitation
to a one-man show at the Goupil, a printed post-card informed
her of the most efficacious method of exterminating rats, a

bill for gas, a courteous note from Mr. Bilsom, the grocer. She tossed them into a heap.

"What a lot of effort," she said under her breath, a clumsy movement, the table rocked crazily, she went down the room, took a seat opposite him.

"Light's very bad to-night," he said, not looking at her, not thinking of the light.

"It is dim, isn't it ? Say when you want your gruel."

The word "gruel" induced some life into the cat : it began to stretch itself, scratched at the carpet, finally began washing its face.

"I thought I heard somebody knocking here a few minutes ago," he said, and rather mumblingly, "somebody inquiring—something——"

"Knocked at the wrong door, looking for some other flat," she said, seeing her again in her mind's eye, petite, a mass of red hair, seeing it under a dim light, hearing the young woman saying, "I heard he was working again. He knows me, Clem does."

"What time is this Doctor Beacham coming ?" he asked.

"Never said what time," she looked in the direction of the horse-hair sofa, "that looks better," she said.

"I—it's a matter of the light, that's all, dear," he said, adding quickly, "oh, I worry about you, dear," crossed to her, held her face between his hands, bent down, kissed her. "I worry about you."

"I wish you wouldn't," she said.

"Did somebody answer that bell downstairs ?"

"Expect so. It's stopped ringing now, anyhow. Say when you want your gruel."

He nodded, lit another cigarette. He thought, "Not dear, not Clem, not Stevens, not Mr., not darling. Just '*you.*' *You* want your gruel, no letters for *you*. Will that suit *you* ?" A half-smile appeared on his face, vanished. "Names," he thought, "never calls me Clem." He looked at her.

"Any news ?"

"No ! Those ground-floor people are still away. I think that airman fellow got a leave. A noisy lot. Must

have drawn blood somewhere. They're very excited. I
heard a girl singing," she jumped up as though struck, "I'll
get you your gruel," she said.

" All right," watching her go, following her with his eyes,
seeing her tall, erect, like a man, powerful, definite.

" Lena ! " he said softly, " Lena."

He heard her pottering about in the little kitchen. Something burning came to his nostrils, he thought, " those
sausages." He got up and walked to the end of the room,
shielded his eyes with his hand, took a focus, noted the
height and length, he looked at the grey curtains covering
the window, his glance swept up the floor, across the bright
strip of carpet. He walked down to the window. If he looked
through he would see a wall, an enormously powerful wall.
He lifted the curtains, seeing the cheap black cloth covering
the dirty windows, hiding the wall, but it *was* there, he
could feel it, the weight and pressure of it. He was staring
at the blacked-out window when she came back with his
gruel. A white bowl on a blue plate, and a big silver spoon
in her hand.

"Here, and *do* eat it, it'll do you good. I want you to
eat it." He went back to his chair and sat down, she sat
opposite, watched him.

"Have you ever thought of Renton ?" she asked suddenly.

"Renton ?"

"Yes."

"He doesn't write," Clem said ; "he doesn't write letters
any more."

" How do you know that ?"

"I know, that's all. I can feel it."

"What about Cruickshank ?"

"Wouldn't understand at all," Clem said, began sipping
his gruel.

"That's him, that's Dr. Beacham," she said, when the
door tap came.

He looked at the clock. "A quarter after nine," he said.

"He can't come in the day," she said, "besides I might
be out."

"Yes, of course," dreamily, "I forgot that," he said.

The spoon clattered on the plate. He stood up, bowl in his hand.

"What'll I do ?" he said, confused ; "what'll I do ?"

"Wait in the kitchen till he's gone. It's only Beacham, I told you he'd be coming. Go on, and eat up the gruel as I told you," she began, pushing him towards the door. They went into the kitchen.

"There ! I've lit the electric, sit down there. Won't be long."

She closed the door on him, then hurried to answer repeated knockings.

"Good evening," Dr. Beacham said, walking right in, tall, red-faced, jolly, beaming with health, smelling of soap, sleek-haired, "this is the best time I can manage," walking down the room, slumping into a chair, throwing his legs out, "quite a job in this blackness, I can tell you, and there seems so many other things to attend to." He rubbed his hands.

"All right then," he said, stood up ; "will you get yourself ready ?"

"I am ready," she said, made a quick movement with her arms, the whole chest was exposed.

He stood looking down at her. He put a finger to his mouth, began rubbing, said, "H'm, ah, yes—yes, I see. Um ! Oh, dear ! Well now."

He was tapping her chest but she seemed hardly aware of it.

"You'll have to go away," he said, "but it's not a difficult matter. How old are you ? "

"Forty."

"Not difficult at all, really. But it'll have to be removed. I'll make the necessary arrangements."

"No."

"But you must——"

"No arrangements can be made at present," she said ; the words stumbled out, heavy clumsy words, she felt she was at the bottom of some high stairway that must be climbed. "I can't leave him."

"But surely he can manage," irritable, protesting, "surely——"

"How would you know that ?" she said, her eyes on his clean white hands.

"He can't be left, it'll have to wait." She covered herself up again, "besides the pain isn't half as bad as it used to be."

She sat down in Clem's chair. There was something ruthless, final in her attitude. "I could never leave him, *never*."

"It's in your interests, it's vital. Something could be arranged for *him*."

"You mean my husband," correcting him, stung by his remark. "His name is Clement Stevens."

"I know that already. I heard the name somewhere many years ago, too."

"So did he," she said, "that's his name, and he's my husband."

He folded his arms, suddenly put them behind his back, clasped his hand together, balanced on his heels, slowly rocked himself.

"I came a long way to see you," he said. "You know that."

"I know. It was most kind of you," she looked directly at him ; "he worried, he has an idea something is wrong, it was to stop him from worrying. Something is wrong, of course, but I daren't go away at present. Perhaps I could go for daily treatment."

"Could I see your husband ?"

"No ! I don't want that. Please. He's sitting in the kitchen, I can't keep him waiting there. I'm so sorry. I'll come and see you."

He saw how excited she was, he thought she looked very tired, he did not like a high colour suddenly appearing in her cheeks. He said, "You know my address, come and see me. I'll write. Make it in the day."

"Let me see you out, Dr. Beacham," she said.

"Not at all, I'll see myself out," he said, smiled at her, picked up his hat and made for the door. When he opened it she followed him out. Suddenly she clutched his arm, said in a low voice, "Of course he knows what it is all right. He's too clever not to know. But he thinks its cancer of the heart——"

"The heart," Dr. Beacham said, "what a curious idea to have. The heart. Never been known. But these kind of people indulge in extremes, jump off at tangents, how silly. But you must have that breast removed." He shook hands with her, said, "Good evening," walked quickly away.

When she heard him going downstairs she went in again, closed the door, then called, "He's gone. You can come out now. He's gone."

He came shuffling out, she was waiting for him by the fire. He handed her the bowl.

"I didn't eat it all," he said, "I wasn't very hungry."

She took the bowl from him, thinking, "The way he came out, the way in which he handed me the bowl. Just like a child." She said, "Go and lie down. No, better still, go to bed. You've been working all day, you're dead tired. I've made everything nice for you. *Do* go."

She went up to him, took his hands in hers. "Go to bed, you're tired."

"What about you?"

"Yes. I'm coming soon," reassuring, "I've a letter I simply *must* write. Is there anything else you want?"

She put her arms around him. They were silent for a moment.

"What did he say?"

"Who?" she said, a note of surprise in her voice, she was worlds away, and then she blurted out, "Oh, of course. The doctor. He didn't say anything very definite. I'm to go and see him one day next week. In the afternoon perhaps. I may be able to manage that all right."

"Was that all?"

She was laughing, laughing in his face. "He didn't agree with your theory," she said, "called it nonsense."

"Why *shouldn't* a disease be new?" he said, watching her; watching her, still laughing, there was something irresponsible, something slightly delirious about it.

"No such thing as cancer of the heart," she said. "In fact it's very, very ordinary, *really*. He said the operation was a simple matter. *Very* easy."

"Operation ?"

"Some time—but not at present. Come along now. Come along."

He followed her up the room to the partitioning curtains, she went behind them ; he said jerkily, "Half a minute." He crossed the room to where the easel stood. "Half a minute." She came out and joined him. They stood there looking at the enormous canvas. He held her hand. She glanced up at him. The expression he wore made her suddenly sad. She put her hands on his arms, slowly turned him round ; he moved like a robot, he was automata.

She said softly, "It's all right," suddenly kissed him. "I believe in you."

He covered the canvas with the linen cloth ; he walked away. They went behind the curtains ; he began to undress. She sat on the little stool, watching his every movement, and only rose when he was in bed, the blankets drawn up to his chin ; he stretched himself, lay still. She went off and returned a moment or two later with the big overcoat ; she laid this on his feet. "It's rather cold to-night," patting where his feet were. She put a glass of water on the table at his side, a little box with some white pills in it.

"You'll soon be asleep," she said ; "you'll feel fine to-morrow."

"Colour's not right. The colour should *bleed.*"

She didn't answer him, didn't look at him. She went away, thinking of sausages in a pan ; they would be cold and greasy now. She went back to the fire and sat down, jerked cigarette stumps into a heap with her foot, suddenly was motionless, looking at the canvas over her head.

He called out, "You there, Lena ?"

"Yes, I'm here. I'm just writing a letter. I won't be long." Half-rose, sat down again, she was undecided, got up again. "Perhaps I'd better," she said under her breath, shuffled down the room to the card-table and stood with her hand on the battered-looking typewriter, finally took up a sheet of paper and an envelope, the pen, and a small bottle of ink ; she returned to her chair by the fire. She wiped fluff off the pen-nib, dipped it in the ink, spread the paper on a piece of boarding, began to write. A blob of ink fell, made a bad blot ; she hardly noticed it, went on writing.

"Dear Flo,

"I got your letter and am so glad to know that all is well with you and yours," she paused ; "how awful about the little dog. I've been trying to make up my mind to ask you if you would be able to"—the pen was in air again, she thought of the country, *all* that green, a garden, a lawn, a field, would ink reach that far, count against all that green, would she—"able to get up for one afternoon, a matter of two or three hours, certainly not more than three at the most"—paused, thought explanations, explanations—"just to be with Clem whilst I'm at the hospital"—the pen was moving, words were appearing on the paper, but she didn't see them, wasn't thinking about them, only about a little dog—"Oh !—what rot !"—hurling the pen to the other end of the room.

She jumped up, the ink-bottle fell, the sheet of paper swished towards the fire, its edges began to curl under the heat. "I'm so sorry about your little dog—about your little —little dog"—began laughing, was suddenly crying— "little dog, little dog, little—oh, God !"

She switched off the fire, walked up the room, took her coat and hat from the nail on the door. She put them on. She looked down at her house-slippers, went back down the room, behind the curtains where Clem was, behind the curtains where Clem slept. But she couldn't see him. The blanket was drawn right up, seemed wrapped about his head. She said, "Are you asleep ?" There was no answer. She turned out the light, and went away. At the door she stood looking down at her slippers. Should she change into her shoes, should she— ? She opened the door and went out, closed it silently behind her, took a key from her pocket and locked it. She thought, "He'll sleep all right," thought, "those pills are good."

She was on the landing. Music floated up the stairs ; she saw the thin pencil line of light under the Robinsons' door, she went downstairs.

Emily was still standing in the doorway of her room ; she heard a man snoring—it would be Mr. Frazer, she thought. She didn't notice Emily, she was quite unaware of Emily, she was being drawn downstairs by two words which made circles round her mind. "Go out ! Go out !" Emily might stand there for all eternity, but *she* must go out. She passed down the next flight, felt cold air coming up ; she tightened her coat collar about her throat, reflected that she might quite easily have changed into her street shoes, stopped suddenly. Was that a light ?

She was sure she had seen a light, as though somebody had opened a door and then quickly closed it. She wondered how long Clem would sleep. She wondered where she might walk at ten minutes past ten in the evening. She wondered whether they would come over again. She was on the ground floor, she was in black darkness. She could hear wind coming up the hall, a pattering sound.

"Still raining," she said. "I wish it would stop raining. That light again."

It had flashed out behind her, somewhere a door had opened, and then she heard a man's voice calling, "Aye, aye, there !"

She swung round. It was as though he had spoken to her. "Of course, nothing matters very much now, *reely*," a woman's voice was speaking.

"Aye, bloody aye," the man's voice said.

Lena heard a giggle. She walked back up the hall, one hand rubbing its surface ; she felt the cold damp of tł is. Surely she had heard that voice before, that young woman's voice. Surely she had—and then the light flooded out. The door had been opened. Lena drew back to the wall, held her breath, a young woman had come to the door. And now she knew.

"Came to see Clem. Said she knew him. Ten years ago. I wonder."

She was looking into a room. A man was sprawled in an arm-chair, a gas-fire blazed up at him. There was a table with a green cloth on it, a full bottle and an empty bottle, two glasses touched, stem to stem. The young woman looked out from the doorway, leaning, hands pressed on the panelling, looking first this way and then the other ; she seemed to be searching for somebody, she was giggling again ; she called over her shoulder, "I don't see anybody here," hiccoughed, "You must be drunk." Laughed outright.

Lena stood quite still. "Came to see Clem. Heard he had started work again. Insult !" He had never stopped working.

That red hair, that face, the cheap finery, the powerful scent, the purse-like little mouth, the snub nose.

Came to see Clem. Used to sit for him. Ten years ago. Rubbish. She wondered if the young woman had seen her.

"Oh ho, yo ho, oh oh ho," the sailor sang, kicked the gas-fire as he stretched his legs, "oh ho, yo, oh ho," slobbering, "come'n have a drink." His every movement was clumsy, he stretched and the table shook, the glasses tinkled, one of the bottles fell, began to roll.

"Sufferin' hell, come'n in, Cis, and shut that goddam door. Oh ho, yo, oh bloody ho."

He was laughing, his big teeth discoloured, a dirty brown, a dirty green, he had a two-day growth of stubble, his enormous hand beat out the time of a tune, he hummed this, suddenly stopped, said, "Oh, Jese."

Lena moved away from the wall, she was standing in the light. She was looking at her who knew Clem. She did not speak. She merely looked. Something you could see through something you could touch with your hand, you had only to put your hand out, something with a mass of red hair, a white blouse that appeared to have a tear in it, the sort of tear that the doll-like hands pressed against the door could never make, a sudden insane tear. Their eyes met.

"Hallo," the young woman said, and the sailor seeing Lena called out, "Hallo there, Cis, come'n have a drink, oh ho, bloody ho," still slobbering, still beating time with a clenched fist.

Lena stiffened where she stood. Words were forming in her mind, were flooding up from some dim fastness, crowding her tongue, her mouth opened, she was on the point of saying, "I thought you had gone, but I see you are still here," but her lips were motionless, nothing came. She turned her back on the young woman, she squeezed her way past the black door. She was in the street.

CHAPTER II

"Oh !" she said, stumbling against him, "I'm sorry." She wasn't really ; you had to say something when you were frightened. She was moving past him, past something she hadn't expected. She had only expected to see Clem. Working again after all that time. She wondered who the woman could be.

"Hallo there," the sailor said, "hell bloody ho," hiccoughed, "your voice sounds like that of—of an—" hiccough, "old friend." He stuttered, he recognized an old friend's voice by a single "Oh !" He was moving about on the floor. In the darkness she thought of frogs.

He was staggering to his feet, for the first time he was conscious of a shivering coldness. "Lumme !" he cried, hiccoughed again, "it's cold. Goddam ! I say there, help me up," hands waving in the air, he was on his knees. "Help me up," he said.

"Come on," she said, put out her hands ; he grabbed ; she caught his coat-sleeves. "Get up," she said.

She felt a weight, he was pressing on her hands.

"Don't be silly. Get up."

His hands gripped hers, he pressed hard. "Help me up. Goddam this dark."

"I'm helping you up," thinking of Clem ; she was helping Clem up, her mind was full of Clem. The little genius.

Working again. Good Lord ! He began to pull, she was staggering, was suddenly angry.

"Oh, God ! Get up, do get yourself up off the floor. You're just a stupid fool."

He felt her hands' softness, he had a purchase. What was next ?

"Must have been asleep. Somebody trying to play a joke on me—this confounded place," he was hiccoughing again, "joke—aye !" another hiccough, "hallo there !" boisterous, hail-fellow-well-met, the voice thundering in the dark hall, "hallo there. I say—where's my bloody matches ?"—a series of wind releases—"who the hell are you ?" He was laughing in her face. "Of course ! Sure ! Goddam it, I know. Recognized your voice right away, voice of an old pal."

She couldn't see his face, but she laughed, laughed at his face. In the darkness she imagined it. Fear was gone. Clem had gone, she was only curious. Who was he ? What was he like ? Dead drunk. Asleep on the floor, in a dark house. She was imagining the face, she felt the serge of his coat, she could see the top of his head, realized he had no hat.

"Where's your hat ?"

"Aye !"

"Your hat," she said.

"I dunno. Where the hell's them matches ?"—broke wind—"excuse," he said.

"You're drunk."

He was upright, bending over her. "Hallo there," he said ; "how you doin', eh ?"

"You're funny," she said.

"Sure ! Where's my matches ?"—abrupt, accusing—"where's my bloody matches ?"

"*I* haven't got them."

He bent down and begain groping about. "Here they are ! Half a mo."

He pulled one out and struck it. He held it aloft. "Hallo there," he said.

She didn't speak, just stared down at something which certainly wasn't Clem. Clem she had come to see, this was only a drunken man, and seeing the blue jersey as the match flickered, "a drunken sailor." Now how could he have got in here ?

The match went out.

"Where the devil am I ?" he said, fumbling with the matchbox.

"As far as I know you're in a house ; it used to be a house, but it's flats now. You were stretched out on the floor. I nearly fell over you," she said.

He stood up, struck another match. He towered over her. She felt his height, a sort of weight hanging over her. He kept on striking matches.

"There should be a light here," she said ; "give me those matches." Taking them out of his hand, she struck one, walked down the hall. She found the switch, she flooded the hall with light. He came up to her, put his hands flat on her shoulders, looked at her for some time without saying anything.

"Where's *this*, anyhow ?" directly in her face, a sort of ultimatum.

The weight of his hands began to tire her. "Please," she said, lifted them away from her shoulders. She noticed some dried blood on his chin. Must have fallen. Perhaps he had had a fight.

"This is Chelsea," she said.

"Goddam ! Where in hell's Plaistow ?" he said, earnest, urgent ; "where's Plaistow?"

She thought, "we can't stand here." She said, "It's a long way from here."

"Put that bloody light out, will you ?" Somebody was shouting down the stairs. " Go on. Put it out."

"Who's that ?"

"Oh, somebody wants the light put out. We better put it out."

"Put it—" hiccough, "put bloody light—all right, put it out."

"Of course, they've been over here once already," she said ; pushed him away, went to the light switch and they were in darkness again.

"What the hell ?'' he growled. She felt his arm round her.

"I'll go,'' she thought, "I'll go now. No. I won't go. Clem's here. I'll see Clem.''

"We can't stand here like this,'' she said, rather fiercely, and, after a pause, "can we ?''

"Cis, you're great,'' he said, was suddenly yawning, "no place you can get inside, no sort of—I'm off to Plaistow, hell's bells.''

"They may be over again,'' she said, wondering if they would, thinking about Clem, about that woman—who was he ?—thinking about Plaistow. Name of a place. Where *was* Plaistow ?—thinking of somewhere to go, to sit, she burst out furiously, "can't stand here all night.''

"Must be some place,'' he said ; fog in his mind was slowly clearing, he belched wind, but she was looking away towards the stairs, up the stairs where Clem was.

"Lumme, there must be some bloody place,'' shouting, "*who'll* be over ?''

"Ssh ! People are sleep. *They'll* be.''

"Who ?''

"Oh, God ! You're drunk. Dead, dead drunk. How did you get here, anyway ?''

"Who's they ?'' leaning over her. "Who's they, Cis,'' but she pushed him away.

He followed her up the hall.

"Don't you follow me,'' she said ; she was angry, a haze in her mind. What *was* all this ? Why didn't she go ? Standing here, talking to a perfect fool. Curiosity exhausted itself. She had better go. She could see Clem any time—that is—the woman rose in her mind, the overcoat flapped at her, woman and coat became a question-mark, the woman was saying in her ear, " *Can* you ?''

She was by the front door.

"Oh, heavens ! It's pouring now. I wonder if they'll be over again to-night ?'' thinking in terms of sounds, "I hope they don't come over again.'' She stood quite still, she shuddered, thinking of sounds. "Oh, God !'' she said.

"Come on,'' he said, "come on, Cis. You're great.''

He was standing over her again, pawing her coat ; she could feel his strong breath, she drew back.

"Come on, Cis," he said.

"You leave me alone."

It made him laugh. "Here, gimme those blasted matches," he said, his voice rising, "gimme the goddam things, playing a joke on a feller, like that silly little bastard threw me in here, gimme them," but the box was already in his hand : he had dragged them from her.

"I'm a sailor-man, Cis," he said ; "anything goes with me. You think I'm drunk." There was a final hiccough. "You needn't be scared of me."

"I'm not."

"That's fine. You're fine, Cis. Goddam, you're just fine." His speech no longer thick, the words had shape, the fog was clearing fast. "Recognized your voice right away."

He left her standing by the wall, he went up the hall again, he struck match after match, he saw a door. He went up to it, he began rattling the knob, he thumped the wood with his fist.

"Hell," he said, "*hell*. Hallo there ! Anybody in ?" holding the match high, seeing the immaculate white door, seeing a wooden plaque on the wall, reading "Miss Benson—Miss Cleate." He rattled viciously at the knob, he thought of the young woman. She looked fine. She had red hair. Falling over him in the dark. Falling where from ? Laughing in his face, telling him they might be over. Who in Christ's name were they ?

"Hallo ! Hallo there," he cried out.

She heard the rattling knob, she heard him banging on the door, she heard him begin to hum a tune.

"I'll go," she said ; "I'd better go."

"Must get some confounded place," she heard him say. The crash that followed made her jump. "Hallo there ! Someone show a bloody leg."

He was in a room. "Come on, Cis," he called to her, "come'n in. Come'n Cis." She only heard the pouring rain, the last bus driving along a drenching, windy road, heard sounds far off, high up, somewhere very high, thought of Clem, here in this house, alive, working after ten years of silence. Clem up those stairs, in that room, and the woman there.

"Come on, Cis," the sailor said. He was at her side, his arm was round her waist, she was moving as he moved, they were moving together towards the room.

"Come'n in, Cis. Hell's fire, you're not scared of a sailor-man, come'in. You're great," he said. "Come on, we'll have a drink." They were at the door, they were in the room. He closed the door, shut it against the dark hall, against Miss Benson, Miss Cleate, airing views in Somerset.

"There we are ! All fine and dandyo. Nobody answered me. I said show a leg there, I said hallo there, I said to my-self, 'bugger me, Jack, this place is empty. We'll have a drink," he said, "nice little drink."

He was behind her, gently pushing her towards a chair. She seemed quite indifferent to being pushed, quite unaware of a sailor ; she was studying the flat.

"There ! Sit down. We'll size each other up. Aye ! That's it, Cis, size each other bloody well up."

He was laughing, standing over her ; he had pushed her into a green chair. "Lo, Cis," he said.

"Hallo," she said, softly, looking beyond him, the furniture interested her. She watched him as he drew a whisky-flask from his pocket.

"There we are."

"Wonder it didn't smash when you fell down," she said. She forgot the furniture, the green furniture, the pale green walls, the Picasso reproduction over the fireplace, the natural oak table with its green top cloth, the bookcase full of books with the green bindings, a green dream.

She was looking at the sailor, noting his size : there was something huge about him, big head, big hands, long legs, big feet ; she looked up at his hair, sandy, thin on the top ; a long face, the nose amused her, the mouth was heavy, but the grey eyes, so wide apart, seemed divorced from all this hugeness, this utter strength, they were so calm, there was something *too* calm about him, they were in the wrong kind of face.

Whilst he was pouring raw whisky into two tumblers, which he had got noisily, clumsily, from a shelf in the next room, she was studying his face, a big pock-marked face, an old fever perhaps, studying his hands, and then again the long face under the bright light. The flask shook in his hand, the glasses tinkled.

"Come on, Cis," he cried ; held a tumbler towards her.

"Here's how. The skin off your nose, Cis," smiling down, his great mouth half open, his right hand held high, the glass trembling, she hoped he wouldn't drop it. "Come'n, Cis," it was almost a growl. "Drink her up."

"I can't without water," she said, and put the glass on the table.

"Hell, no. Should've got water, should've," a fugitive hiccough was bravely held back, stemmed down ; he drank his whisky at a gulp, he banged the glass down, went out, later came back with water in a jug.

"Good heavens ! The *jug's* green," she said, burst out laughing.

"Eh ?"

"Nothing," she said ; took the tumbler. "Well, here goes." She sipped at the whisky. She left the glass balancing on the side of the arm-chair.

"You're fine," he said.

"Am I !" looking at the Picasso reproduction on the wall. "H'm ! You're drunk. You've had far too much."

"Sure," he said, "sure I'm drunk, a sailor-man don't get drunk by proxy."

"By what ?" the final word intrigued her, "by what ?"

"Proxy. Know what proxy is ?" He came from behind the table, was smiling down at her ; she saw his teeth, a broken one, a green one, a glitter of gold. There was something warm, even endearing about that smile : she could feel the warmth, at the same time was a little afraid of it.

"By God," he said, "you got some hair, Cis," his free hand was on her head, the long, thick, insensitive fingers running through the red mass.

She said nothing, she only felt the hand running through the hair. "Sure, you've a fine head all right," he said, looking at the small features, the snub nose, the mole under the chin, her big eyes, the small mouth, the white throat and the well-developed chest, the long black coat that hid something white. He suddenly thought of the gas-fire, of heat.

"Oh, hell, I forgot," he said, pressed a switch, the gas-fire blazed up at him, made hissing sounds ; he sat on the table. "Have another," he said, looking over at the half-empty flask, "have another." Her glass toppled to the carpet, the whisky spread, made a stain.

"Holy mackerel," he said, "you gone and spilled it now," bent down and picked up the glass. "Say," he said, laughing, "you seen a ghost, Cis."

She didn't hear what he said, didn't notice the tumbler falling, didn't see him smiling at her, she was thinking of sounds. She thought she heard them now, far distant, faint, but the prelude to thunders ; she sat up suddenly as though struck, remained motionless.

"What's the matter ?" he said, "goddam it, you're coat's singeing."

He stood her up, he removed her coat, flung it into a corner, laughed. "Oh, hell, you're tight. Sure, you're tight all right, Cis." She heard the words, they passed into her mind, they froze there.

"They're back again."

"Who's back again ?"

"*They* are. I can hear them."

"Christ Almighty, who are *they* ? Come on, Cis, you want another drink."

He poured whisky into a glass, he was generous, it was like water. "Here, drink it, drink it all up, that's a good kid," hand on her arm, his hand was on her breast.

She pushed him away. "I'm not drunk." She sat down. Colour returned to her cheeks, strength came back. "I thought they were over."

"Yes, but goddam it, *who* ? "

"Who d'you think ?   I'm not drunk, needn't think I am," coldly.

"Look here, Cis, we seem to be quarrelling or somethin.' Hell's fire, I'm just a common sailor-man.   You're scared of me," laughing at her.

"I'm not," laughing back ; she was poised, she was without fear, she had only imagined those skyward sounds.

"I'm not drunk," protesting.

"Get drunk. Goddam, get drunk," he said. "I got more. Plenty. Trust a sailor-man."

"Suppose somebody came in.   Suppose the people who live here came back.

"That'd be fine. I'd say hallo. Sure, we'd all have a drink. See !"

She sipped from her glass, she kept her eyes on him. "He's awkward in this place," she thought.

"I suppose you lost your way," she was saying. "So did I. Easy to lose your way nights like this. I came to see some-body, and I couldn't see him. I came a long way in the rain. It's rained all the damned day, it's *still* raining.   I was going back where I live and I stumbled over you."

She put the glass back on the table.   It was empty.   "Who are you ? Where are you from ? Where are——"

"Well, I like that. Why, I'm just a sailor, Cis. I lost my way. God's truth, some feller pulled me off the ice, and here I am. I was all in, I was scared stiff."

"The ice ? "

"Sure—the bloody ice."

She was astonished when he shuddered.

"Aye, I hate ice, Cis."

"Ice. Now I know you're drunk," she said.

He flung his glass down : it smashed against the gas-fire. "Ugh !"

She was filled with horror.

"What's the matter," trembling, moving back in her chair, "what's—" it was like the sounds had come again, flooding, down-pouring sounds.

"They're over again," she shouted.

"Don't laugh at me," he said, "I said *Ice*. He got me off the ice, a crawling little bastard of a man with a helmet. I'm scared of ice."

"I'm not laughing at you," she shouted back. "I'm not, not laughing."

He was trembling. She wanted to jump up, she wanted to go, now, to fly, to forget him to forget Clem, to forget a green dream. And suddenly she was out of the chair.

"Let me go," struggling to get past, struggling to go, struggling to forget.

"Half a mo," his voice shaky, "half a mo. He shouted at the top of his voice, "No, no," and desperately, "no, no don't go, don't go, don't leave me," clinging to her, all his weight against her weight, his hands moving up and down her arms, he shook, he was clinging, holding on to her. "Don't be scared, Cis, I'm all right, only scared of ice," he said.

"I'm not scared," she said. "How calm his eyes are," she thought, "how calm they are, still——"

"All right. You're not scared." He picked up the flask, put it to her mouth, he poured raw whisky down her throat, "you're not scared," his voice was tender. "I wouldn't scare you," he said.

She broke free, he grabbed, the blouse tore, she was past him, she was by the door. He went after her, he held her tight. "You're not scared," he said, "I wouldn't scare you."

He took her back to the chair, he made her sit down. He went and sat in the chair opposite her. He did not look at her, his eyes roamed about the green walls, glanced at pictures, bright colours, odd shapes to him, the glass case with crockery inside, books on a shelf, a long green carpet, a white door.

"At first I thought this was a ship. But it's no ship," he seemed slightly disappointed. "It's a room, and somebody must live here. I wonder who that feller was, chucked me in here. What the hell's this place, anyhow? I live at Plaistow. My name's Johns."

She left her chair, crossed over to him. "I'm not scared," she said.

"Sure ! You're not scared. My name's Johns. What's yours ?"

"Celia Downs. I came here to see somebody I know."

"Hallo, Celia," the sailor said, "shake," he held out his hand.

He held hers. It was light, soft, small, it was lost in his, he hardly realized it was lying there. " 'Scuse my paw," he said, grinning at her.

"All this's damn queer to me," he said.

"What ?"

"All this," swinging his arm, indicating everything, all the green ; "must've been dead tight all right, must've been fuzzled, dreaming, but I thought I was on the ice again."

"I wish it was light," she said. "I could go home. You could go to Plaistow."

"That's it. Let's have a drink," suddenly noticing the tear in the blouse, the rise and fall of a breast, the pinkish skin. "Let's have a drink."

"No thank you," she said.

He was surprised, he suspected.

"You're getting scared again," he said.

"I'm not scared, I said so."

"Oke doke. We'll have a little drink. Who'd you come to see ? Let's talk."

He made her comfortable again in the green arm-chair, he went out to get whisky. He knew where whisky was, like Miss Benson did, Miss Cleate, airing themselves in Somerset. She heard him moving about in the back room. He returned with two bottles of whisky, one bottle of rum, three bottles of Volnay; he couldn't read the labels quite clearly.

"She's a great ship," he said, laughing, all teeth, he banged down the bottles on the table.

"This is somebody's flat."

"Sure ! I tell you she's a great ship. She got a goddam fine store."

She thought of people living here, she had seen the names

on the board outside the door—Miss Benson, Miss Cleate.

She thought of them, of the rain outside, of the wind through the big hole in the wall, of coming to see Clem, she thought of the sailor dreaming of ice. She thought of how you couldn't be surprised any more, not by anything. She thought of the towering walls of darkness outside.

Her lips moved, she seemed on the threshold of a smile, she was looking down at her blouse, she was inwardly smiling, she was back in an old time, she was sitting for Clem, she was nineteen and a half. She suddenly laughed to herself. She was listening to the sailor. "You're fine, you're not scared any more." She was thinking of Clem.

"Didn't half like my bust, Clem did. The little genius."

The sailor was humming a tune, but she wasn't listening ; didn't hear the popping of a cork.

"Bloody fine ship," the sailor said ; "a *real* sort of a ship, plenty to drink, sort of makes you forget the ice."

"They may come back," she said. "You better get another glass, you smashed yours—remember ?"

He wasn't difficult, just awkward, clumsy ; she wasn't afraid, he couldn't be dangerous, only simple. Lost his way. People did lose their way, especially on these nights ; lived in Plaistow. Merely a name. Where was Plaistow ? She had never been good at geography. Plaistow was a sort of geography. She could hear him stumbling about in the back room.

"I wonder what time it is ?" She was fidgety in the chair. Was she dreaming ? Sitting drinking, talking to a sailor, in a green room ? He came back with a large-sized tumbler. Laughing, he said, "Say when."

"Good Lord ! Stop !" she called out, the tumbler was filling with raw whisky.

"All right," he said, quietly, some thoughts had cooled, "if you want water in it," he filled his own glass. "Hate water in stuff, like sugar in tea, milk in coffee——"

"You've even got a palate," she said, thought, "yes, Clem would like this sailor." She was standing up, leaning over the table, she took the glass from him.

"Palate ?"

"Yes, you've got a palate," she said.

"Oke doke.   The skin off your nose," he said, "by God,"
he said, "it's Irish, mellow, smell the peat in it."   All the fog
in his mind had cleared away.

"I thought you were drunk.   Good health, Mr. Sailor,"
sipped cautiously, it might be poisoned, she averted her gaze,
looked at the cheap Picasso reproduction over the mantelpiece,
it completed the pattern, made whole the green mood.   She
asked herself why Miss Benson Miss Cleate were so keen on
green.

"You're fine," he said, "you're not afraid of me, are you ?"
remembering the smashed glass, the shudder that could not be
held back, the tearing blouse, her rigid attitude at the door.

"Let me go," she said.

He was feeling his way out of cross-currents.   He looked at
green things, but he would not see them her way.   He began
laughing.

"Bit like the jungle," he said, "only wants a tiger, a few
leaves," banging the glass on the table.   "I like you," he said.
"I heard you say something, I forgot, something about—tell
me," he said, leaning over her again, but she did not feel his
weight.

He was sitting on the table, hands flat, gripping the edges,
she saw for the first time a small tattooed star behind his
right thumb, she looked at this for some time.   He was gently
rocking himself.   Then she looked up at him.   His eyes
were still calm, a little pool of clear water in a dried-up river
bed, somewhere in the East, the sun burning.

"Tell me something," he said.

She was laughing, green dream gone, Clem gone, rain had
ceased, wind died down, the last bus was quiet in a garage, men
washing her down.   There was silence, high up, higher than
the roof, high as heaven, there was silence.   She was calm.

"What'll I tell ?"

"For the first time she giggled, and he liked that, it meant
something to him, he knew what giggles were, and it made
him smell sea, ropes, think of docks, ports, women, plenty of

women. They all giggled, now she giggled.

"Anything. Half a bloody mo. I got it now," suddenly excited, as though he had solved a problem, discovered the root of x^2. "You came to see somebody—man, I'll bet."

"That's it," unconsciously crossing her legs, he noticed this, he thought she would giggle again. Everything had a technique, even a feeling.

"Oh !" he said, looking away towards the door, "I see," a slight, even forced laugh, "oh, dear," and quickly, the most vital, the most urgent thing to be said, this very minute, "you're not scared of me ?"

"Not a bit," feeling more herself, "I came to see an old friend. And you ?"

He said nothing. She watched his slow-moving mouth, he must be trying hard to say something, watching the thick red lips, the blood on the chin, it made her think of a hippopotamus, a mouth full of mud, a great mound of mud rising up, the hippo waking, spouting mud, he was like that to her as she watched. She said abruptly, "Say it, get it off your chest, sailor."

"I like you, you're fine." His hand was on her head again. "Likes me," she thought, "good heavens ! Likes me. Easy with a sailor." Suddenly she wanted to ask a question. "What about the ice ?" but she could not, remembering the shudder. "He should be home in Plaistow," she thought.

"I like you fine, Cis," he was saying ; she saw how quickly his expression had changed. "I like you."

A longing there, a discovery, a revelation, something soft, lovely, under his eye, he had better look *long ;* he wanted to drink her up, swallow her, something he had to remember, "to get right inside you," his eyes were wide, devouring her.

She thought, "Now, if I look in I will see right to the back of them."

"She's fine," he thought, "she's good."

Something pretty, bright colours, something sort, sort of velvet, after dark places, hardness, after granite, cold rocks about, seas, ice on your nose, scalp freezing, he was trembling violently.

She got up. She knew. She understood. She flung her arms around him, she kissed him, the words came at last, but she did not speak them. She just thought, "he has a horror. He has a horror."

Warmth was in her, going out to him, softness like light playing on dark areas, breaking down the hardness, cold contours of worlds, "he has a horror."

He felt her, he held her, tight, he felt warmth, the softness, there was no sea smell, he thought of a bazaar in Egypt, he smelt that. His mouth opened. She put two fingers against his lips, the thick, lost lips.

"Ssh ! Don't speak," she said.

He forced her head back, his mouth was on her throat, he kissed her. His hands were in her hair, he was pressing her back, he was slipping from the table. She didn't know he was slipping, she looked up at a white ceiling, "this, too, should be green."

His hand was at her blouse, opening, his head was there; he slipped easily off the table, they were staggering on a green carpet. He held her, mouth pressed at her throat, tight, pressing hard.

"Oh, Cis ! " he said. "*Oh*, Cis ! "

She saw a livid scar on the top of his head. She didn't move, didn't speak. "He has a horror," she thought, "a horror."

"I love you, Cis," he said, mumbling ; he would not take the lips' pressure from her throat, would not remove the hand that took the weight of breast. "I love you," he said.

She wanted to laugh, it was funny. She wanted to cry, it was sad. Lost, lost in a green dream, a jungle. Loved her ! He loved her. Clem came, Clem came out of a door in her mind. "He has a horror, Clem," she was saying, "he has a horror."

They swayed, they were still.

" I love you, Cis," he said, "you're not scared of me. I love you." His hands were suddenly moving up and down her arms, it made her think of snakes. "I love you," he mumbled on her white throat, "love you." And th n it was out, spoken, over, done with.

"You're afraid of something, you have a horror," she said, but he made no answer ; he was thinking, thoughts didn't matter, only the softness, the warmth, something was melting, he could feel it going, rising out of him, flowing away, into a cold wilderness, and he said softly, so softly that she did not hear it, "it's gone." But she was quite still, she would not move. She didn't want to.

Slowly she raised his head up, looked at his eyes. She heard him say, "It's gone," she heard him shout, "Gone."
"What's gone ? "

"The ice. Have a horror of ice. Always something moving under it. I know."

"That's good," speaking quickly. "I'm glad."

"His horror was ice," she thought, "he remembers ice."

He was moving, she was moving, he was pushing her, against her back she could feel the table's hard wood, he was pressing her back. " I love you, Cis, I love you."

The blouse open wide, the breasts bare, rising and falling, his hands there, his body pressing, pressing, she was being pressed back over the table. She felt his breath. She shut her eyes, her hands stretched out to find a grip, the green cloth had swished to the floor. She wouldn't move. She wouldn't speak. She smelt whisky in his breath, she would say nothing, do nothing. After the cold, warmth, after the ice, fire. She couldn't think of it in any other way but this ; life was like that, patches of light, then dark, the silvery bay, the barren reef, a man as lonely as a whale. The words falling out of his mouth, the light shining down on her closed eyes, the big mouth, the lost lips, the blood on the chin. Words pouring out, a cataract, falling on her face like scalding rain.

"Poor sailor," she thought, "had a horror—now it's gone."

"Tell me about ice," she said.

His mouth was at her ear. "Ice," he said. "You said they'd been over. I said who are they ? You said they might be over again, who's they ? You tell me who they are and I'll tell you about the ice."

She opened her eyes, he was smiling down at her. "God ! You're great," he said, mouth pressing to her mouth ; she pushed him away then.

"The bombers," she said, suddenly cold all over, they made her feel like that, a cosmic coldness, mysterious, terrifying.

"Oh ! Those goddam bastards," he said ; began laughing, she could see right inside his mouth, a plate holding three teeth, one gold, some green, the rest a dirty brown, "civilized on the inside," she thought.

"I never worry about those bastards," he said.

"You tell me about the ice," slowly rising, pushing him back ; she was suddenly thinking about Clem. "Didn't half like my bust."

He let her sit up, he looked at her bared chest. "Not scared ? " he said.

" Not of you. Tell me about the ice. Go on."

"What about a drink ?" he said.

"That's fine, let's have one."

He went away, left her standing against the table.

"What say, how about that fizzy stuff ? Gassy, makes you belch, though."

"No ! Whisky," she said. "I like whisky."

He poured it out. "Still want your water ?"

She nodded.

"O.K.," he said, and quite involuntarily, "should be in bloody Plaistow." He gave her a half-tumbler of whisky and water ; he filled his own to the brim, raw. "First to-day, Cis." They drank.

"Ah, no," he said. "I don't want to talk about goddam ice. I'm happy."

"You get it off your chest, sailor," she said, "you'll feel better."

"By Jesus," he said, "you're fine, you're swell, you really are bloody trumps, Cis. Aren't scared of me. Goddam, I love you, kid, I do honest; ain't scared of me ?" the glass trembling in his hand again, the right arm round her shoulder, something soft to feel, pretty to look at, after the long crawl over ice.

"No," he said, "I don't want to say anything," a little gruffly, "why'd you keep bothering me, Jese ! I'm happy, sure, I'm fine, you're fine," leaning over, kissing her again. "I was on a goddam ship"—stuttering—"ah, bugger me, Jack, I won't—no, I won't." He drained his glass, he put more whisky in it, he drank again, some spilt on his chin. It made her laugh, she hadn't heard anybody swear like that before, like a new language.

"The way them things shake when you laugh," he said. "What ?"

"Oh, hell—nothing, Jese ! I like looking at you. I love you. Yes, I do."

"Go on," she said, "get that stuff off your chest."

"Oh, it wasn't a horror," he said, the tone was full of apology, something he shouldn't have mentioned, not important, didn't matter.

"By heck, this is a room, eh ? Wouldn't half mind a f'c'sle like this. Is it still raining ? I ought to go to Plaistow."

"Where's Plaistow ?"

"Some goddam place," he said. He was pouring whisky into her glass, into his own ; she didn't notice this, he didn't ; the bottle shook violently, whisky spilled on his trousers.

"Smell," he said, "real *stuff.* What's a bloody horror, anyhow ? Here's how, Cis," a quick kiss, a fugitive peck at her mouth. "All right," he said, "touch. That's fine."

They clinked glasses, they drank. She was a little unsteady, she was suddenly seeing Clem, and then she hurled the glass against the white door ; he didn't hear it smash, "no, no more," she said. He didn't hear her, drinking it back, getting warmer, warmer, after the horror, after the ice. He put his glass back on the table.

"Hallo, where's yours ?" Then he saw the fragments by the door, the green carpet strewn. "Hell's bells, I like that. Wasting it, wasting, wasting the damned stuff, real *stuff.* Never mind. You're fine. We'll get another glass."

"What about the ice ?" she said ; her speech was thickening, "what about the ice," her mouth half-open, but he didn't notice this. "I came here to see——" He wasn't there, he had gone into the back room. She staggered to her chair, slumped down. He brought another tumbler in for her.

She was full length on the green carpet. He felt her rigid against his touch. "Here, come on," he said, "you got the hebe jeebe's or somethin'."

"The ice," she said, "tell me about the ice."

"Goddam the ice," he said, "come'n have a drink, come'n have one."

"Tell me," she said, closed eyes.

"Nothin'," he said, "nothin'. Colder than cold," he said, "hard, like iron, shoving along, two-thousand tonner, no man's ship. Neptune's bastard, shoving her along into a nor'-easter, freeze your guts. Spike was on top, his name was Spike, good skipper, sure, knew his job, shoving her over. When the horn blew we knew what the horn meant——" He stopped suddenly, looking down at her ; she was motionless, white-faced under the light. "Ah," he said, "ah, to hell with it." Looked at her again ; she made no move, she seemed hardly breathing. "Listening," he said, "she's listening."

"We were up, out, slithering, falling, getting up, falling down again, Spike always shoving her over, towards a bay whiter than any snow is, we could see it. 'See him ?' Spike shouted from the bridge, sure we saw him. 'A black sod,' Spike shouted, spitting ice bits, not breath, 'up there, see ?' Sure we knew, we saw the sod, blacker than hell, circling over, circling round, going high, higher, coming down, down fast— darkness was crawling up on us, he came along, whup ! He smashed the wireless, he went away, darkness came along quick. 'Got to get that fixed,' Spike said ; sure it had to be fixed, getting near the bay, whiter than snow is. "A man to go up there,' Spike said. We knew what he meant. I was leaning on the rail then, bosun came by. 'A man up there,' he said, "quick.' Then quicker than quick he was climbing up, darkness came right in, feel it coming over, sure. Spike shoved her along, all the time he was up, high up, truck top, had to mend that wireless, had to shove her along. Spike

knew, we knew.'' Pausing, slobbering a little. ''Hours up
there, maybe, four, five, couldn't count, ice everywhere, in
your guts, freeze what you thought, sure, colder than cold,
like steel, rock, you know, that hard.   May be seven hours up,
you try counting, you feel ice bits in your head, you stop
counting.   Spike kept her going, shoving her along.   Unfreez-
ing at the bogie we were, bosun come in the fo'c'sle.   'That
man ain't come down,' he ses, 'better go up, *you*.'   'Sure,'
I said, 'sure I'll go up.'   Had to relieve him, might forget
him being there, thinking how froze up you were.   'All right,'
I said, thinking about up there, thinking I'd like that hot
bogie in my guts.   I went out.   'Ought to have had him down,'
I said.   'A sub makes you forget a lot of things,' the bosun
said.   I was going up the mast.   Spike was shoving her along,
all the time, sure he knew his job.   I was climbing then, I was
near the top.   'Ah, this buggering cold,' I said, and then I
was up where he was.   I said, 'Aye, aye.'   I said, 'Hallo,
there, Brown, where you got to, eh?'   Stuck my fist out,
lost it in that dark.   I climbed again.   'By God,' I said, 'I
can't hang on here.'   I shouted, 'Aye, aye, where the hell
are you, Brown?'   I saw him then.   I knew he wouldn't say
aye, aye, wouldn't spit any more.   I was at the truck top.
I could see his legs, feet round the mast, sure I saw that.   'Aye,
aye,' I said, talking like that, easy, but it didn't matter, froze
there, legs froze, face froze, arms stretched out reaching for
somethin', hands feeling for something, ends, picking up ends,
what the black sod smashed.   I didn't say aye aye, I just
looked at him, made you think of Christ, two pieces of wood.
I slid down.   'This bloody, *bloody* war,' I said.   I got to the
fo'c'sle.   It give me the jimmys.''

He stopped.   She did not move.   ''Have a drink,'' he said,
hand on her hand, he looked at her closed eyes, white face,
her lips moved.

''Tell me about the ice,'' she said.

''Jese !   I told you, Cis——''

''Tell me about the——''   Saying this, she was sick.

''Couldn't say anything twice, kid,'' he said, slobbered,
''that's the bloody way I am,'' leaning over her, something

wet splashed on her face.   She did not feel this, his face was pressed to hers.

"God, you're warm, Cis," he said.   "God, you're warm." Something wet on her face.   She was sick again.

"Don't be scared of me, Cis, I'm only a gutful of swears. God, you're warm."   Hugging himself in, feeling suddenly cold, thinking of ice, seeing it rise, white, then bluish, towering, great walls, sheets, layers, a world of it, blue, shining, cold, silent, where no man was.

CHAPTER III

SHE squeezed her way through the black door.   She was out.

"Oh," she said, "how good the air is."

To her full height she stood, motionless, breathing night air. Darkness reeled, she was still, she was a still column in this. Darkness rose and fell, like waves, swept forward, engulfed what you could touch, what the eye saw, the wall's shape behind her, this too, engulfed.   As when one moves seawards to bathe, apprehending the sea's touch, so adding conscious weight to prisoning clothes, she had come down, she was on night's shore, she had the touch of air, the feel of it.   As one strips for the sea, the unsure foot testing the extreme edge, so she was stripped, so things were falling from her, now, as she stood still in the black desert, at extreme edge of a reeling sea.   She felt the weight move, she was feeling it go, falling, feeling it fall, bric-à-brac of hours, rust of days.

"How good the air is, how good," beginning to move, moving, "I'll go this way."

Slowly, unsurely, getting the feel of this sea, feet apprehending voids, where no voids were. She put her hands to her hat, she wondered if it was straight.

"How dark," she thought, increasing her pace, getting the sea's feel.   "I hope he sleeps," she mumbled, "they say those pills are good."   Saying this he was risen in her mind, life-size, he was with her, he was where she went, stopping at

street's end, she knew this was the end. Darker than dark,
yet she could see. She turned left. She knew this road, it
was long, it was a quiet road, always had been quiet, in a
noisy world. She liked this road. Darkness obliterated shape
but she had the feel of it, often in the old times they had gone
together, had sat in a quiet garden under elms.

The light of a passing car dazzled, air seemed to shake
long after it had passed by. Suddenly she stopped, was
uncertain, undecided, her mind said, "this far but no farther."
She turned round, looked back through columns of darkness,
towering behind her.

"No ! I'll go on, a walk will do me good. I wish he would
walk, but he won't go out, now."

A foot-fall was thunderous, the outstretched hand a white
blob, trembling as leaves tremble under wind.

"Along here, I believe I know the place exactly, there's a
seat. I'll go further along, it's not very late, I'll sit down."

She walked on, and somewhere behind, like the echo of
her own foot-fall, Clem's. She moved inwards now, knowing
where railings were, where a wall was, she found this seat.
She ran her hand along, it was filmed with damp, but she sat
down. It was their seat. She could not see elm, shape or
shadow of elm, but she felt it there, upthrusting from hard
winter ground, lost in this black, rolling sea. Clem had once
drawn this elm, life-size in her mind, there to touch. Clem
was there, too, by her side, she could touch him with her hand,
and she saw the face, the small face and the grey hair at
forty-three, the snub nose, the mouth that always seemed to
her to have a wilful look, she often thought Clem was his
mouth. She saw the light brown eyes, the small hands, ugly,
but powerful. She saw Clem.

"The road gets narrower as one moves on," she said, as
though he were listening. Thinking how suddenly the road
in their lives had forked, they had to slacken their step, they
had to go slow. Five floors up in a grey house, that's where
he was, five floors up was an eyrie, somewhere where you
could work.

"I know it'll be good, yes, I *know* that," and she was with him, five floors up, hand clasping his hand, standing together looking at the canvas. "If it were not good I would have told him."

She turned her head quickly, as though she had heard a sound, was listening for others, but she was only looking away, back through dark columns, these fell, darkness was pulled down, she could see that house. See the door stood up, hingeless, see behind it, the long stairs, the fifth one smashed, she could see a going-away morning, for two grey ladies who liked green things, who went off in a smart car, both dressed for Somerset air. And on the next floor the laughter, the music, the crying child whom you never thought about, never even knew existed until Bolivia went off the air, the only station his wireless would ever get. Robinson the name was, he was in blue, air force, machine-faced, how he could laugh. Laughing, they would never stop, she knew this who had been drenched by it, Clem and she in the cellar's dark corner, and the laughter there, laughing, that's what they could do, fill a house with laughter, send it soaring to the fifth floor where he was, where he worked, cursing the light, wondering if the colour was right. Laughing as she passed their door, as she came out, they would be laughing when she returned.

She got up, she went further along this road that she knew so well, hurrying now, a desire to reach its end, to go further and further, thinking of this laughter, not giggles, not guffaws, just outright laughter, cascades, showers, roulades, floods, endless, a kind of wrecking power in this laughter, you could feel it. Her pace slackened, all this laughter was gone, her step slow, she was on the next floor, thinking of two who were old. Frazer the name was, you could hang a label round their necks, "Lost." Behind the screen of fear they remembered a world where doors would close, the magic touch.

A clock was striking, she stood still, she counted the strokes. "I'm sure he'll sleep, those pills are good : Beacham said so," herself laughed. "Cancer of the heart ! Well I never." She thought of Flo. "If she could get up from all that grass in Essex, she could see to him," whilst she went to the hospital. Instinctively she turned right, she did not falter, she knew this world, these streets, these roads. A black sea and how cool it was. A quiet sea, and you could think. You had to think since the road narrowed, the road forked, you had to think of him, of them together ; you had to think of an end.

"The world is drunk with shouts." You thought of shouts, you heard the word "future," you thought, "how heavy the mortagage on this."

"Oh !" she said, "oh," her heart leaping.

"Excuse," the man said, "this infernal black-out."

"It's all right," she said, walked on, her body still feeling the jolt, his footsteps died away.

"If I turned right here I could cross the park," and she was turning right, she was moving towards the park. She drew strength from this quiet, black sea, strength to go on, without tiring, strength rising as she went, she was full of it, she could travel far and she would not tire.

"If I go to the bottom of this little street, then cross over, I'll be in the longest road of all. I wonder what time it is. I wonder if he'll sleep. I wonder if Flo *would* come." Suddenly thought of her chest," doesn't hurt now." Perhaps the pressure there was of a kind that Dr. Beacham could not diagnose. Perhaps Clem was right, a new disease, an illusive germ, the slide waiting for it, it could not be filed. She felt for the kerb, she suddenly thought of the young woman who had called. Celia her name was, said she had once sat for him. But *had* she ? And that sailor, poor fool, to whom everything was jungle unless it smelt of sea, was water, salt. Together in that room, drinking.

She crossed the little street, turned right, she was in this road. Somebody crossed behind her, walked level with her, but she heard no sound, felt nothing, looking ahead, getting the feel already of the damp breath, great walls of it rising up from the city's tongue, she was thinking of the river. She knew the river, she loved it. Hands lightly clasped in front of her, a loose hold on the coat, not feeling cold, nor air's damp, just feeling it come nearer, coming stronger to her nostrils, the river's smell. Head bent slightly forward, her pace easy, casual yet certain, a focal point, a definite object, the walk towards the river.

"This walk will do me no end of good, I wish he had been able to come."

But he hadn't and there it was. Still, she could take back a freshness to that room, she could carry home a river smell, an hour's walk, she could talk about that, about a coolness their room would never own. She would mention the seat, the elm behind. She stopped, threw her hands into the air, made a little staggering movement, as though without realizing it she had reached precipice edge. No precipice, only light, a mass of light falling, darkness rolling back before its white flood, shapes looming up. The moon had come from behind heavy laden cloud. She stood quite still, she was like a swimmer who, diving from a great height, surfaces in temporary confusion of mind. She was like that.

The light had come, the black sea was rolling back, back as far as she could see. It was too sudden, this drenching light, those patterns of street, hole, corner, and road. An unsought revelation, it was too sudden, it was too much. The dark sea had seemed more secure, this was only brazen, cold, struck at the eye, burrowed in a mind's fastness, resurrected hours, time striking, a handless clock grinding out hours, because a cloud moved, because a moon shone. She raised her head and looked round, then she walked slowly on.

Past and around shapes she walked, the river's smell stronger in her nostrils. If the moon went, it would take shapes, the dark sea cover the phantasmagoric, the galvanic nightmare frozen by light. If the moon would again become lost in cloud, these shapes would go. But it was full, and clouds were sailing fast to the west. Eye could rest or sleep in a dark sea, but here it was fish open, it could not close, could not close against the forest of shapes, towering and tottering, turning and twisting, the frantic reel, forcing eye's total power, it could not rest, eye opened wide, horizon was endless, emanations of broken hours, you could not shut them out. Moving as she moved towards the river's great breath, its long shining tongue, Clem lost, house and black door lost, elm and canvas lost, Flo and the chest's pain lost, the pressure ceased.

The pavement suddenly widened, she moved in towards some railings, she saw a bench, she stopped, looked about her. "I'll sit here for a while, I don't think I want to go any further. I wonder what the time is." Drawing her coat collar tighter about her neck, sitting hunched up on this bench, not a sound nor a step heard, behind her a staggering wall, behind this she remembered was a little red church, she turned right round. She was dwarfed by the shape, a drab brick pile, an eyeless window, a demented stone pillar holding up nothing. "I felt safer in the darkness, I was warm in that black sea." Rising to her feet, hesitant, questioning herself, "Shall I go right to the river or shall I go back?" She wondered. "Perhaps he'll wake, perhaps those pills are not so good. I wonder if I should go back."

Moving a step, turning, drawing back a pace. "It was the air, the air was so good. No, I'll go on. I'm sure he'll sleep all right." She thought how much a face would count now, a face to see, turning a corner, moving down on her, a human face emerging from this welter and frenzy of shapes. She walked on, she passed by the little red church fallen, a red giant flat. She could see a grey stone building to her left, it was not standing, it could not stand as buildings stood, it hung, like draperies hang, and the next grey, and one of bathstone colour, and these were hanging, all draping sky. She stopped. In a world of suspended motion a sudden movement. You had to look.

She looked, she saw a balloon coming down, slow, elephantine movements ; lost, isolated movement in a still world, you had to watch. It was like something out of another time, you thought of an undiscovered sphere, a new kind of mammal. Coming, lower, lower. She was at the corner of a short street, she knew it would descend here, she had to see this touch ground, she knew not why. But it must touch ground. She looked up ; she saw its shape. She hoped that round a corner, out of a hole, down a street, across a road, she might see a face, and she saw this.

Lower, so reaching roof level, lower and suspended between houses, then touching ground. Something enormously swollen, a bugaboo. She watched it settle, shiver, it was still. Gigantic rubber ears, they looked like ears. Come down from a great height, trailing ropes, and then she saw a face, a man's face. Seeing it, near to her, under a helmet, violently red, very close to her in moonlight, she saw it red, weathered like leather, but she did not think of the face, only the balloon. Two small eyes were peering at her from under the steel helmet, she was unaware, she was staring at the balloon. A human face that was red, a moment ago she would have warmed to it, but now she could not, a red face in a quiet street, not a step heard, not a sound moving, not a word spoken, and behind it this yet quivering mass, the thing descended from the spheres. She looked at the mass, she thought of prodigious lice, white lice.

She moved on, she was very near to the river, she could almost hear its flow, water lap against wall, she was suddenly thinking of swans, white as this moon, tumbled home and snug on river's surface. She crossed the road. She saw the river, she was full of the river. She leaned on the wall, looked down on a quiet strength, breathed in what this great flow exhaled. Drenched in smells. A long white ribbon, flowing under a still moon. It made her think of a small house, of them together in the beginning days. Flowing behind a city, under a city. The same river they had watched together. Watching it smooth flowing, a girdling strength, round streets and buildings, round walls round people, children, round those working, those asleep, round them together as they watched, in an old time, those beginning days.

"Poor Clem," she said, quite involuntarily; she hadn't meant to say it, it jerked out, a jack-in-the-box movement, like that sudden electric flutter of swan's wing, there, under her eye, as though this bird had dreamed, like a tossing fragment whirling by. Words had been like that. She leaned, she devoured the river, she drew up, sucked in its smells. The small house came clear, the bright future, the buoyant hours. "The river," she was saying suddenly, "the river," like a child's hurrah, a sudden smile, somebody saying, "I'm *glad*."

She had always loved this river. How often they had walked up and down, always watching its flow, like a duty to do, like a salutation. Stretches of strength here, great stretches, years of it, deep in city's bone, deep rooted. Strength. You leaned far over, you put your hand in, you felt strength, miles and years of it, it sank deep in bone. She felt a coolness again, she could feel this as she had felt it outside the black door, in the wide dark sea. She spread on hands ; the wall, closed eyes. A small house with a green door, flowers in a box, bright blue curtains.

"I am with Clem."

. . . .

He went up three steps and opened the little door, the sun followed him in, his shadow danced, the house was flooded with sunlight. He closed the door, went down a short corridor, he came to a white door, was suddenly cautious, silently turning the door handle, pushing it in noiselessly, he did not go right in. He looked in, peering, he saw Lena. She was putting first bluebells in a stone vase. He followed her hand's movements, he looked at her face in profile. He enjoyed this look, it was not often he caught her disarmed, poiseless. What a strong face, it seemed more masculine than ever looked at in this way, something earnest, a belief there. Then she turned as though divining his thoughts, she looked towards the door. He held his breath, wondered if she had seen him. He had a horror of being caught like this, still entranced by the expression upon her face. He knew he would never get this in any other way, no miracle, no magic hold it, he would never get it on canvas, never. He pushed open the door.

"Hallo, darling," he said, and as she jumped, "sorry I frightened you ; didn't know you'd be in this time of the morning, thought you'd be shopping. Did the phone ring ?"

She dropped her hands to her sides, her lips moved, nothing came out, she shook her head, the shake of the head said, "telephones do not ring."

"Post gone ?"

"Gone," a heavy falling word, lead.

"Oh, hell," he said, and she knew the anger, she could not think of bluebells in a stone vase. She said, "Nothing happens," her inward anger stronger than his own.

"Something will, dear, believe me, something will," eager, earnest. She half-smiled, this became a laugh. "That's ten years old. Like Corney's whisky."

His hands were on her shoulders. "You see I *have* to tell myself this, have to believe it, have to drive myself. Life's not short, as you think, there's time, something will happen. I saw Rupert this morning," jerky words in the air, the atmosphere could not hold bluebells in a stone vase. She was moving, she was going out of the room.

"Wait, Lena ! Do sit down. I have to explain, do wait," hands round her neck, pleading, "darling, something *will* happen."

He made her sit down.

"Tell me what this man Rupert said," spreading her hands on the chair's arm, trying to relax, knowing she could not do this, eager to listen, knowing the words were old, the sounds the same.

"Well now "—looking straight at her, looking hard, wondering what she was thinking, hoping she would understand, ten years was nothing really, he was sure she would.

"I told him he could take the two paintings Burt has, and that personally, I didn't object to his sense of values, in cash terms, not this morning," rather fiercely, so that she drew back in the chair, wondered if he had had a drink, almost on the point of saying, "I wish you wouldn't take drink when you've nothing in your stomach."

"I can't value anything this morning, dear," watching her face, a white face, a beautifully plain face, wondering if it would light up, waiting for it to suffuse into some sort of life. "Oh, for Christ's sake, don't look like that, don't you understand ?—that's all I can do NOW." Now was a very long word, dragging the tongue's length, an enormous word forcing its way out through the small mouth, "I can't do anything—*now*."

"I don't want to stay here," she said, "it's no good," she said ; she was rising from the chair, she was suddenly crying.

"Oh hell, Lena," he said, her face pressed to his coat, her mouth crushed there. "Perhaps it's better not to talk at all. Let's forget it. Oh God ! Let's go out," unconscious of the fact that he was shaking her, "let's go out," half dragging her towards the door.

"Wait a minute," she said, "wait Clem," and he was wiping her eyes with his handkerchief.

She kept looking at him, in the most suspicious way, there was no other way she could look, still wondered if he had been drinking.

"Let's go out, just to the door," he said, whilst she half-turned, looked disconsolately at flowers lying on a table. "Oh, damn them," he said, "come along, dear," pulling her after him. She did not resist. They were at the door.

Sun was on them, they felt warmth. He opened the door, they went down the steps. They did not speak. It was like a pre-arranged plan. They crossed over the road, and leaned on the wall, looked up the river, looked down. And then she was looking one way, and he another, standing quite still as though they were frozen into positions from which they could never escape, as though great distances were between them, a sprawling desert. Looking away from each other, back to back, in silence. She looked at swans, she thought of swans, her head was full of a whiteness.

"I saw that bloody hopeless fool, Gorton, too," he blurted out, not moving, and she did not move, nor question, did not seem to hear.

"Said my exhibition was now out of the question. Said there would now be plenty of work painting dragons, and, though dragons were fierce, they paid plenty of money, I told him he could go to hell," savagely, hurling the words into the air, like speeding bullets, but there was no target.

She had not moved, she had not heard. He still looked towards the west, and behind him a human phalanx, continuously moving, sheer weight behind him, moving along, some fated ordination at work, they seemed to be moving in

one direction.   But he still looked west, looking at the river,
a riot of movement, of sounds, of tremendous energy.   Ships,
barges, flats, rowing-boats, swimmers, sea-gulls, a forest of
preening swans, but he saw nothing of this sprawling life.
''Lena.''
No answer.
''*Lena*.''
No answer.
She was not leaning on a wall, not looking at a river, she
was not with Clem.   She was in a room, lost in a big arm-
chair, broken-springed, she was stroking a cat, unconscious of
the cat, in a room that was cold.   He had gone out, this,
their first day together.   But the room was word-choked,
atmosphere electrified by them, chaotic, and now they were
falling into some kind of order, she could see them coming
clear.
''You might have told me.''
''What.?''
''About this.''
''About what ? ''
''This,'' her hand sweeping air, her hand in one encircling
movement, embracing coldness, cat, and decaying grandeur
of another day, the dilapidation, the things that looked mean.
''All this.''
''You knew what to expect, d'you suppose I like it ?''
''I don't know.''
''It's all one vast bloody struggle,'' he said, and then she
was sorry, she got up.
''I'm not afraid,'' she said, ''I was doubting, but now I'm
not. I believe in you, Clem. I mean that, I'll stand by
you.''
He was laughing.   ''You are a darling, really, you see if
you went away *now*, I'd be done.   I have to lean on you, I
have to know you are there.   All this rotten façade, this—
rubbish—it's just the crazy machinery of struggling along,
never bothers me, *really*—and it won't bother you soon,''
still laughing, ''just now you'll hardly notice it.''
They were one, embraced, they were resolved, nothing

mattered now except this, being together, holding, and then he said, "Hold on, Lena."

"All right."

"I'll go and see Rupert."

"Don't be long—please don't be long," and quickly, "couldn't I come ?"

"No ! Don't come. I won't be long."

The door banged. She threw the cat down, reckless ; she went into his room. She sat in a chair, this was the room where he worked. She looked at pictures heaped against a wall, disgustingly abandoned, one on an easel, budding hope. And the smell of paint, and the disarray, the tubes, the brushes, the ash, the torn letters, the infinitesimal fragments, the half-burned cigarettes, one isolated splendour of cigar, unsmoked, untouched, how she hated this one lonely cigar. Sitting here, it might be a cage, a prison, a humming hive, energy, endless hope. She went to the wall, leisurely looked at canvas after canvas, smiled at a signature, something fierce about it, a thumbnail insanely scratching in the bottom left-hand corners, S.

"He works ; God, he works."

You could work, you could say something, you could see where to climb, to fix what you said, you could see a clear flight of steps. You worked from bottom upwards, but suddenly this staircase was spiral, it had no end. You worked on, somewhere there was an end to these stairs, somewhere you could stand. Silence was long, had a leaden weight, so that you could feel this as you worked, from bottom upwards, you knew there was somebody about, someone in the forest of rounding stairs, someone who would watch. You would work on, and suddenly you came on him, he spoke, and you laughed, silence was broken, you had met one who understood your language.

．　　　．　　　．　　　．

"That was—how long ago—how many years—one—two—doesn't matter, it was just years, a long time," muttering to herself.

She stood back from the wall, feeling a shiver coming on. She began rubbing her hands. "I came out for a walk and just look where I am."

For the first time she was laughing. In front of her was a bridge, she had not noticed it until now, a bridge ; it had been one of those demented shapes, hazy, a kind of fog there, and now she saw it quite clearly. So she laughed, laughed and exclaimed, "Good Lord ! It's only half a bridge," she went on laughing, "half a bridge."

Standing there all that time and she hadn't noticed it. A clock struck, she listened, counting strokes. "I'd better go back now."

She thought of him worrying about her, he might wake up suddenly, those pills be quite useless, she hated the thought of his worrying about anything—now—he had that work to do, she thought that enough. Half turning, she stepped forward, she was going back to Clem, then stopped, she must look again. She had a feeling that she must look at this bridge, shock of surprise was still with her, and the cold shiver did not drive full home. Her hands were pushed up the coat's capacious sleeves, she turned round, she looked at this bridge.

You had to look, you might never see anything like it again, a bridge that began on stone foundations and ended in space, a half-arch, it wasn't really a bridge, it was a gesture, an attitude, a feeling of desparate reaching forth, as though it *must* reach that other side. It was all wrong, the bridge should go right across. Here it was, not steel, not stone, just a wooden gesture. What could it be but an act of frenzy, thinking of men building it in a crazy hour, these curves and sweeps of wood, reaching out, trying to get to the other side of the river.

"I was staring at it all the time, yet I never noticed it."

She turned and moved off down the road, crossed over where an island stood, increased her pace when she got to the other side. She knew it was late, she had been out too long. She felt she had only been thinking of herself, not of him. Then she was shivering, it came right home.

"Stood there far too long, no wonder I'm shivering. I hope

he slept all right, that's all that worries me now.''

A car flashed by, a bell rang, she hardly noticed it. ''This walk has done me good.''

If only he would come out, but no, he would not do that now. He would not come out. He would not stop working.

''If only he would come out,'' suddenly sad, thinking of him five floors up, refusing to move, it made her feel sometimes that he might never come out any more. Something had happened to him, she knew this, knew it in this moment, it stood erect, bold, you could not shut your eyes to it, something had happened to Clem.

How that stand by the river had driven home a time, something she had long forgotten about, something to which you never gave a thought, since all thought was on pressure, the pressure now. Not on her chest, that was nothing, a momentary irritation, a mere itch.

''My God ! Something's happened to him. Now, I know. Yes, now I know.''

You thought of days long past, you knew how quickly you would forget this, you had to think of pills, vinegar, bandages, this was the pressure you felt.

''It's good, I know it is. I believe in him. Once I didn't understand at all, didn't know what strength was, didn't know what he meant. Now I know.''

Rupert came into her mind, Rupert, Clem's brain child. Never even existed. How she had laughed when he read that obituary notice, supposedly from *The Times*, but it wasn't. It made her laugh. ''Died, privately, at 18, Holme Place''— where they lived. How she had laughed, had been a little angry with his lies over Rupert, who had bought nothing, Clem borrowing money from somebody he christened with that name. It didn't matter now, it had made her feel bitter at the time, for Clem's sake.

Grinding, grinding along. Through years. To-day he could again paint dragons, they were all the rage ; you could get money for this, but he had never been good at dragon paint-ing. She was cradled in these thoughts, her body seemed to gently rock along under them, they carried her forward, round

a corner, down a short street, across another road. She
stopped.

"The elm where we sat, the elm Clem did. I wish he
would come out, but he won't."

You couldn't do anything about it. She went on, she
would soon be home. She would go silently upstairs, she
would be asleep before he realized anything had happened.
He hated her going out, too.

"It's this pressure," she said, "it's this pressure."

The moon disappeared behind slow-moving cloud, she was
in darkness again. The black sea coming up, surrounding,
filling street and house, covering hole, corner, and road. To
some this would be a sudden blindness, signals down, directions obscured, but she knew, she had the feel of it. She was
in her own street.

"It's done me good—still—perhaps I shouldn't have
gone," feeling the benefit of air, after the crushing heat of
five floors up, full of misgiving, "if he has waked."—"I'd
better hurry," she thought, and suddenly, "There it is—
there it is !" she said.

A sound coming up river, she could feel it coming behind her.

"There it is," she said, a sure foot faltering, beginning to
grope, as though she were a stranger here, as though this sea
of darkness were wilderness, the feel, the sure touch of it
going. A sound could do this.

"He'll wake, he'll hear it, it's all begun again—again,"
talking loudly, as though she were addressing audiences, "it's
not far now," trying to hurry, not hurrying, feeling frantically
in her pockets for the torch she had forgotten all about, why
on earth hadn't she remembered it ?

"Here it is, in my pocket all the time," switching it on,
throwing a cone of light forward, across this sea.

"Oh !" she said, and there it was. The house door. "At
last," she said, squeezing in, afraid this door would crash
outwards, and the sound behind her, coming up, it would
grow louder, it would swell.

She was through, she was in the hall. She was hurrying,
bumping into the wall, against the stairs, the torch light

was drunk. Hurrying up five flights where he was. "I hope those pills made him sleep."

A long sound, deep, you could measure the length, depth of this. You knew it would come, but it was not music, nor any bird's cry, nor that of stone. You listened, you were not surprised, you couldn't be any more. You waited, you knew this sound would spread, rise and fall, make ever widening circles, you knew this mentor of your time, of a city's time. It could not belong anywhere but here. You thought of a far-off region whence it came its substance spun from there, the dementia region. You hated it, yet unheard you would feel insecure, you would feel lost. It was your day, your hour, your watching eye, your third hand. You knew this, climbing, climbing five floors up to where he was.

There was no place this sound could not reach, yet it could not be touched, you felt it behind you, pushing you up, up quickly to where he was, pushing you, a thing, yet you could not touch it. You thought of city's loneliness, it might be that cry, and then you said, no, loneliness has no voice, never had, never could have. You said, this is an emanation. Rising and falling, pouring in, far spreading sound. Some sort of cry from stone, those strangled shapes ? Perhaps a cry from these, pride sucked from their bone. All the songs in hell sung, all the sounds known, but you could not name this sound. A lawless sound, outside all music.

She reached the top of the house, sound still following, feeling in her pocket for the key. "God," she said, "he's awake, no pills could drown this out," swollen, torrential sound, filling house and room, flooding stairway, deluging sound. She put the key in the lock, but as she turned it, the door opened of itself. "That's odd," going into the room, calling, "are you all right ?" No answer. "Are you there ?" going down the room. She saw him then. "Did you sleep ?"

"No ! I woke up after a few minutes."

He was standing with his back to her, there was a handkerchief round his head, she smelt the vinegar, said, " Is it your head again ?" Thought, "Oh, God, I shouldn't have

gone." "Your head paining again ?" putting her arm round
him, who did not move. She thought how weak he looked,
looking at his back, but then people often did look different
that way ; she wished he would turn round, say, " Hallo."
She saw the brush in his hand.

"Have you been working ?" doubting it, knowing he
would not work except with daylight.

"I must get this down," he said, not moving, not turning to
look at her, as though he were talking to somebody outside
at a great distance, as though she were not in this room.

"Yes, all right. I went for a breath of air. Are you all
right ?"

"Yes, I must get this down," shouting, "*down.*"

She knew. She said, "Yes, all right, but it may only be a
false alarm."

"I must get it *down*," he said.

"Somebody's been here ?"

"Help me to get this downstairs."

"All right. Who's been here ?"

"Then do come on, Lena, you know I won't leave it here,"
suddenly excited, waving his hands, the soaked handkerchief
fell off his head, shouting, "Look ! Woke up, I got that,
see !" Clapping his hands, "Got the *depth, there.*"

"Who came ?"

"I must get it *down. Now.* Help me."

She wondered who had been, what had wakened him, she
was looking at this enormous canvas, echoes and feelings and
stress of other journeys coming home to her. He would not
go any place without this. Once she would have laughed—
an idiosyncrasy—an aberration—now she would not laugh,
thinking of wilderness of roads, mountains climbed through
years, falls, obstacles. Yet he had said nothing, he had not
raised his voice, he had just gone the way he knew, done what
he believed in. So he believed in this, so this was part of him,
so they would go down together to the cellar's darkness. She
would help him, who had shown her each strand of strength.

He turned round, took her hands in his. He said, "Lena !
Hallo, Lena. You went out. I woke up. I always wake up if

you go out without telling me," then anxiously, squeezing her hand, leaning towards her, suddenly kissing her forehead, "Are you all right, Lena ?"

"Yes," she said, "I'm all right, Clem."

Clem ! Warmth to him, this, saying, "Clem." "Help me down with it, Lena."

"Who came ?"

He was nonplussed, caught out, he stared at her, said robot-like, "Somebody came, I never noticed." He was looking beyond her now, at the door. A man was standing there, he wore a helmet, he had a fierce, harassed look.

"Better get down there," he said, "they're over. Better get down," and then was gone, his quick run down carpetless stairs making a series of thunder noises, stopping on each landing, calling loudly, "Better get down, they're over."

"Come, we'd better go," she said, "I'll help you, dear," leaving him, going to the bedroom for his overcoat, his tweed cap—he never would wear anything but a cap—his mask. Getting their thermos, the handy sandwiches in newspapers, vigil might reach as far as hunger, a great thirst, you never knew.

"Here ! Put your coat on."

"Lena," he said, "Lena," soft in her ear.

"What ?" rather sharply.

"You think it's all right—I mean—now, if you look at it from here," and she looked, and something screamed down past them, but they didn't hear, intensely looking, canvas sprawled on easel. "You see, the depth's right now."

"Fine, I knew you'd get it, you have such patience," then sudden commanding tones, "come along, now," the quite changed voice, the shielding one, the tool of a long apprenticeship used on others, when the going was hard, the hard side of her he did not know, the raised screen whilst he worked, whilst he waited for the telephone to ring, the post to come, whilst he waited for the right light. And suddenly she wanted to cry. She knew what was wrong. She knew it now.

"Everybody down" an upwards shout, darting into their room. "Ready ?" she said.

"I'm ready."

"Right then." "I wonder who came," she was thinking. "All right, lift," then as weight grew, "*lif*—t."

"Yes, I'm lifting, I'm lifting—I wonder who came," lifting, the easel creaking. "Those pills were good. Somebody woke him up. I wonder who came."

"Somebody," he said, "he hadn't noticed," he said.

"No, he doesn't seem to notice things much, now." The canvas free, the full weight under them, moving slowly, in the half-darkness, the twilight of a new time, moving slowly along, thinking how that walk had done her good, how glad she was she had got back just in time. It always gave him headaches now.

"I wish sometimes he would come out. It would do him good."

"You all right, Lena ?" he said, the voice under pressure, the weight heavy on his arms, "you all right ?"

"Yes, go on."

Moving bat-like, downwards, counting each stair, you would reach the cellar soon.

"Somebody came, I wonder who it could have been ?"

Not Beacham, not Flo. Essex grass pulled too hard, she would never be certain of Flo. "Wait a minute," she said, "wait a minute," stopping, pulling backwards, that pain in the chest again, Clem's "cancer of the heart." She cried, "Stop."

"All right, but I must get it down."

"Yes, yes, I said all right," breathing heavily, "oh, of course," she said, "*that* one might have called while I was out," aloud, "*that* one."

"What ?"

"Nothing."

"God, will you hurry ? you know I must get it down," he shouted behind her.

"All right, now. Go ahead," taking the weight again, not thinking of a cellar, of what you could hear in the darkness there, not thinking of Flo, of Clem, remembering *that one* who called. Said she sat for him. Said her name was Celia.

"Careful Lena.",

"Oh, God ! All *right*, I'm being careful, dear. Said her name was Celia."

.   .   .   .

"Everybody down," Richard said, thinking of Gwen, "everybody down," thinking of her in the cellar. "Blast it ! Would come over to-night." Something bumping into him, something soft. "Hallo, there ! Who are you ? That you, Gwen ?"

A giggle. "It's only me."

He switched his torch on. "Who are you ?" he said ; "how'd you get in here ?"

"Walked in," another giggle.

"Somebody broke into that flat, did you see a sailor in the hall ?"

"Eh ? What's that ?" hiccoughing.

"You'd better get into the cellar," Richard said, "and don't bloody well giggle. If something hit you, your giggle'd be cheap. Go on. Get down there," pushing her, ."oh, hell," he said, catching her as she staggered, she was sick.

"That damned sailor," he said ; "come on, I'll carry you down. You were with him, I saw you. Broke into that flat. There'll be a row."

"Eh ?—oh—I dunno, oh, yes I do"—stuttering—"thass it. Where the music is."

"Come on, don't be silly. Where'd he go ?"

"Where the music is," heavier on his shoulder now, he carried her down towards the cellar.

"There," putting her down, "keep quiet, and no damned nonsense, either. Are you there, Gwen, dear ?"

"Yes, darling, I'm all right."

"Comfy ?"

"Yes."

"Not scared—well, I mean—you're all right ? I'm off any minute now. But I must see everybody safe first."

"I'm all right, really," she said, out of a dark corner, and her voice was shaky, he groped his way to her, they clung together.

"Chin up," he said.

"What's that ?" Gwen said.

"Oh, somebody sick. Drunk—young woman. Don't know who in hell she is."

"I was going to say—" Gwen said, speaking to Richard, who was going, "I——" but he was gone. From the cellar floor heavy breathing came up to her.

"Are you all right there ?" Gwen asked.

"Eh ?"—giggles.

.   .   .   .

She didn't know, she was thinking of Clem. How she had seen him. It was funny, made her laugh. Made her sick again. She remembered this. She was moving from the green dream, moving with the sailor, out of heat, out to fresh air.

"You'll be all right, kiddo," he said to her, "you're fine," getting her out, into the cold hall, a sudden blaze of light on the higher floor, great waves of music from Bolivia.

"Somebody enjoying themselves, kiddo," he said, "let's go up."

They went up.

"You never told me about that ice, you said——"

He was laughing. "Struth kid, I told you that, sure, let's go up. I like that kind of music, don't you," laughing, pulling her back, so their going forward was slow, so this light seemed it could never be reached. "Gosh, that's fine. I like a tune," pushing her up, they were on this landing, Bolivian music drenching them.

"Hell's fire, I heard that goddam song in Peru, sure."

"Hallo there ! Who was in Peru ?"

A blue man looking at him, "Peru, come and have a drink."

"Sure," the sailor said, "so long, kiddo," kissing her, "you're fine, I wouldn't hurt a hair on your head, I love you, Cis," laughing loudly, hand clinging to hers. "Gosh, what music ; *Christ*, it makes you sad."

"Come on, have a drink, I got Bolivia again, come on," blue arm pulling him on, pulling him as he looked longingly after Cis, she was fine, calling, "So long, Cis." Blue arm pulling.

"Oh, sink her," the blue man said, "she's a tart," pulling, he was in. "Here's a fellow likes Bolivian music, darling," shutting the door, the sailor under a bright light, blinking, a young woman in a chair, a baby in her arms.

"Hallo, there, why hallo there," he cried, stumbling forward, "hell-bloody-lo."

"What are you drinking ?" the blue man said.

"Goddam, that's fine. Anything, sure, anything. How's everybody. Aye-bloody-aye."

.   .   .   .

This door was closed now, the higher stairs dark, she clambered up, arms out, hands spread, feeling stairs, feeling dizzy, wanting to be sick, dreaming green. She was at the top. She walked along. She was at the door where Clem lived, the little genius. She knocked, she knocked twice, swore loudly, belched, finally kicked the door. This opened. He was there. She saw him. She laughed.

"Hallo," she said.

"Hallo," he said, turned round, went back into the room, left her, forgot, he went to the easel. She followed into the room. She watched him stand in front of the canvas.

"After all them years," she said ; again dizziness, she flopped on a chair, she might be sick again.

Watching him, the focus cross-eyed, this Clem was dancing a jig in front of an easel.

"Hallo," she said, "hallo, Clem."

He did not hear. He was very busy ; she saw his hand moving.

She sprawled. "Don't you remember me, Clem ? sat for you years—ago, oh yes, didn't half like my bust, eh, little

geeney-wenius, didn't half like my——'' He was painting,
he was jigging in her focus, he had a bun on his head, this
danced, this was bandage, she wondered what made it smell.

She got up, staggered to where he stood.

"Hallo."

He didn't hear, he had no time, he was painting, he was
holding a white handkerchief round his head.

"Are you sick?"

She clutched at his dressing-gown, "Who's *she*?" slobbering a little.

He did not answer, there was no time, he had got it, now.
Got it. Depth.

"You are a—" hiccough "—stuck-up little thing," belching, a burst of laughter, and she was staggering, feeling
lightness of air in her, clutched at nothing, she went staggering
backwards, stumbled, arms threshing air, she trod on something
soft, this spat, she said, "Ugh!" She had always hated
cats. You didn't notice this, it might be an ornament, an
inanimate object crouched before the electric fire, raging heat
in a hot room, on that too bright carpet, a live cat in a room
which Lena always thought was cold.

Aiming a kick at the cat she fell on her back, giggled again,
and then sat up, looking down this room, and there he was,
still dancing jigs in front of the canvas, but the something
white had fallen from his head.

"Doesn't remember me—bloody little—geeny-wenius,"
the critics always said it wasn't right, this wasn't, that, the
other. There he was. Working again after all that time. She
leaned back against the wall, she stuck out one arm, she
touched something, it had an old feel, something she knew,
intimate as her own limbs ; she touched this, then turned her
head, belching again. That fizzy stuff, what did he call it?
The green room *stuff*, the jungle stuff. She didn't look at
him now, it didn't matter, besides he had no time, she only
gabbled against sealed-up ears, he would not hear anything.
She looked at what her hand touched. It was canvas. A pile
of canvases against the wall.

"Lor——" she said, "oh, lor!" Another giggle from the

generous well, glancing at one canvas, then another. "Lor."

She took one up, laid it on her lap, she looked at this, cross-eyed, a man on a chair leered up at her.

"Ugh—lor !" putting it down, picking up another, something that looked grey, she dropped this like a stone, taking up another one, looking at it, it blazed, yellow, blazing corn, a woman making stooks.

"Good Lord !" and then a gasp. "Ooh—I—well *I* never," giggling, "here's *me*," calling down to him, "Cle—m, here's me," putting the canvas flat, staring down at this. *Her* ! There she was, not smiling, not drunk, there she was. "Ooh—lor," herself looking up, half-nude. She was laughing softly, "always liked my bust, Clem did." Hand to her own, feeling it, it was still there, a sigh, she seemed greatly relieved by this. "Colour—thass it, knew what colour was— Clem did," calling out, excited, in between two belches, calling, "Cle—m—here's ME," trying to rise, falling, holding the canvas up, "Cle—m—here's ME."

She was on her feet, waving the canvas, reeling to where he was, standing very still, hands listless at his side, a brush hanging down, staring at the easel.

"Cle—m—O lor !—Cle—m," standing behind him, the painting tucked under her arm, holding it tight.

Something you had found, something she had always liked. She knew. He was a geeny-wenius, *she* knew.

"Cle—m," waving this canvas, letting it fall, dangle heavy in her hand, looking at his back, his head, then she went round, looked straight at him, but he didn't see her, he was looking downwards at his canvas ; she looked, too, and now she laughed at it, she shouted, "Hey !" like a sailor man, "hey ! Here's me," making a complete circle round him again, seeing two Clems, still laughing, "Here's me."

"Hallo, Lena," he said, not thinking of anything except distances, of distances which were important, now these were rolling up like black films, thinking that this sense of distance was going from him. He did not see her.

The canvas waved over her head. "Here's me—Cle—m. You're drunk, too," she said, "ha, ha !" A laughter burst,

"Can't see me"—tittering—"can't see me—I spy."

Slobber round her mouth, Miss Benson's whisky was good, Miss Cleate's. He said it was *stuff*, he knew. "Oh bloody," she said, "oh bloody—look—I spy," both arms high over her head, canvas, waving again, "you've got the heebe-jeebies, he said you could get them"—a violent hiccough —"d'you remember—Cle—m ?"

"All right, Lena," he said, "I've got it. *Depth.*"

"Well, I never," she said, gripped the canvas, held it in front of him, when he said nothing, she pressed, he would feel it against his nose.

"*ME*—stuck-up—little bastard—who's *SHE ?*"

"Mind, Lena," he said, "I want to look again. The depth came. *There!*"

She drew away, she turned her back on him, she went reeling down the room, suddenly sat heavily on the floor, she saw these canvases. You couldn't count, there were too many. She ran her hand over the pile, she looked at herself, flat on her lap, she liked her bust, touched what was real, it was still there, her bust ; this was reassuring to her, who could only see two smiling breasts on this canvas, no other part of her body. All there. He did them, he always liked that one he did of her, always liked it. In a sort of way it *was* yours, you were on it, he couldn't have put it there without you, you thought that way, in between belches, lightness of air in you, strong desire to be sick. This canvas would dance under your eye whenever you looked at it, but that dancing was caused by *stuff*, Miss Benson's, Miss Cleate's *stuff*, she was thinking green again.

"Poor Clem——" her mouth opened, these words fell out, the mouth hung, too heavy to shut. Dead fish-head, gaping.

All these, and there they were, like furniture, or bric-à-brac heap, something swept up, pushed away, obstacles, leave them there. You couldn't count them, they just piled.

"Always knew he was a geeny-wenius."

She knew. When you were like that, like Clem, you piled them up. You pushed them out of the way, making way for pressure of a new one, always there was something behind, pressing it out of them, they were like that. Not counting, not thinking, just working, riots of energy, he had been like that. So here was one she liked, it was from this pile, dust pile, yesterday's ghosts. He would not miss this—miss *one*—besides she had always liked it, it *was* her, her head and shoulders, arms, her breasts, part of a belly. It *was* her.

"Here's ME," could not be heard, a name, Clem, this too unheard by him, he was sensing distances, inwardly laughing at depth he had got. Colour bled, that was right, he had it, he was happy now, who always had liked a particular picture he had done, a girl, nineteen and a half, a beauty from Shoreditch litter, this could sometimes happen.

He liked this one, always had, twice he had had offers, six times had, and he was deaf to these, so he would never sell this, never, who had forgotten it, forgotten her, who had lost it somewhere in a heap, against a wall.

He would look at this wall, but this heap was forgotten, wall was part support of this room, something on which he sometimes flung brain pictures, so he would get certain measurements for canvas work.

Lena had touched grind, more than one day, yet she was always with him, she would touch the bare bone rather than that this went. So it was there, lain many a month, a year.

And now Celia had found it, after years, herself nineteen, who thought, opening a blouse and touching with her hand, that what she touched was of that time still, nineteen, and all youthfulness there. This could come from fuddle-headedness, from the generosity of a man who had seen ice, come from stuff.

She liked this picture, holding it tight. One of many forgotten, one of many you could not count. In a way it was *yours* as well, his kind never cared. You did it, dropped it down, another must be done. He wouldn't know. She would take this, he wouldn't even think of it, and besides, in these days nothing was certain, anything might happen to it. Thinking in this way a right grew, a moral right of sorts, you clutched tightly at this. You would go, you would leave this room, a very long room, always they liked long rooms, leave it, a wilderness with a puppet in it, jigging in front of an easel, leave the vinegar smell, sight of a cat's hunched back, at any moment it might spring.

She got to her feet, a series of gigantic efforts, but she was up, the canvas *feel* helped, sort of pushed you erect. Who Lena was wouldn't matter now, she had this, what always she had longed for, longed for because he would not give, longed for against his hard core of determination, never to sell, but she did not know this.

What he felt a warmth for, a special thing, warmer than blood. Others did not matter. This *did*. It had held off foragers, patrons, the keen-eyed who had the long term view on something that was *good*, the extra something in it, like a sudden view of unknown altitudes. Against the pressure of these through years, which could not break affection's strength, his and Lena's joined, against this, hers was light, it needed no effort. You just tucked it under your arm, and though fuddle-headedness from grey ladies' whisky, and thought of ice-crucified men clouded moments, you never lost the feel of the thing, that you wanted, what you could take, carry staggering from this room, holding it tight, being sure.

It *was* you, you loved it, always had wanted it, you *had* it, you could hang it up, you could admire your breasts, but not his "geeny-wenius," which was in altitudes you could never see, the spirit's meanness could never melt under the feel of it, you had it, nothing else mattered.

She made clumsy strides towards the door, she clutched canvas, clutched handle. Then she turned round again and looked down where he was. She looked at him.

His hand moved, he drew back a little from the canvas, he was sizing up what lay on the easel. She did not say anything, there was nothing you could say against sealed ears, nothing you could think of saying, you just left, taking with you the vinegar-smell, a little frenzy from this room. She opened the door and went out, it banged behind her. It was dark, walls of darkness through which she could not see. She reached the banister, caught hold of this, felt dizzy, was again sick, holding on to what was really *yours* as well.

Sick, and below somebody shouting, "All down. Down below there, please. They're over."

"Oh, lor——" dragging herself erect again. "Oh God !—they're over," the cosmic feel, the coldness, the *utter* feel.

She moved away, she went very slowly downstairs. Then half-way she stopped. She was thinking. She sat on a stair. Always in these houses there was a place under stairs, a secret place, where you could put things, stand waste-paper baskets or garbage for dustmen. She would go there. Still holding her picture, she trod heavily, unsurely down, feeling cold, feeling afraid, because they were over, but still going down, down, where she could hide this.

"Here it is ! I can feel." Fuddle-headedness was leaving her, lightness of air in her going, mind's haziness drifting off. It might be from *having* this sure hold on what was really part yours, it might be because "they" were over again, but her head was clearing, belches ceased, she exclaimed with a child's delight, "It's here, here it is."

She crouched in, she put the canvas down, she felt under the stairs where it lay. No-one would look here for something you could sell, get good money for. She felt it, *twice*, it was there, safe. She crawled out again, she was in the dark hall. A light flashing out, her face in the cone, somebody saying, "Who are you ? Who the hell are you ?"

"I'm ME," a last fugitive giggle, "I'm ME."

"What are you doing here ?" words hitting her in the face, "you best get into the cellar," not hearing what he heard, a down-thrusting scream making you jump, something "*they*" could do by a finger's pressure on buttons, "go on, you better get into the damned cellar."

"Eh ?" and then you staggered, you were caught by arms, you were sick in these arms.

"Hell ! You're drunk," Richard said, and he carried her down steps.

You were carried down, you felt this man's strength, but what you thought of most lay under stairs. You would get this when the light came. You would get money for what he left against a dusty wall.

CHAPTER IV

In a dark corner.

"Are you all right, Gwen, dear?" Richard said, feeling warmth of her, "sure you don't want a light. Just say."

How this warmth got you, sucked at you. He wondered how he could ever get away from it, the warmth of Gwen, but he must go. If that whistle blew, go he must.

"I'm sure you'd be better with some sort of light, darling, *really*."

"Listen to them," she said, "just listen," the voice quaking, she heard drones.

"My God," he thought, "how *can* I go out?"

Gwen laughed then. "Heavens! Listen! Got a snore like an elephant, darling."

"Yes, dear," squeezing her hands, "she's dead drunk. Some cheap piece got in here. How, I don't know. She was in the Benson flat with that sailor——"

"What sailor?"

"Oh, some sort of sailor fellow got in here, fell over him coming back from patrol, flat on his back in the hall, singing. That's another thing, like to know just how he got in here— sure you'll be all right. I must go as soon as I hear the whistle."

"Pray it won't, dear," Gwen said.

Catchword! How easy it came to you, how easy, and then he was hating himself for the thought. "Well, anyhow, their flat's a nice mess, broken glass everywhere, pinched the old ladies' cellar, looks like it, anyway; half a dozen empty bottles on the table. No wonder that thing over there snores." He *could* hate that thing, hate it without really knowing why. "There'll be the heck of a row over that flat, they're fussy you know, may be back any day from Somerset. Left the door wide open, and the lights on, fire burning away. I switched everything off, shut the door. It's all right now— *sure* you're all right, Gwen?"

"Yes, really. Honest, darling. Don't worry about me. You'd better go up and help the Frazers ; better see if Mrs. Robinson is coming down, it's a shame, and that child there."

"Yes, I better do that," Richard said. "Lord ! One gets sick of the whole thing at times. I don't mind what's coming down *now*, it's what may come after, fire—oh, hell, just listen to me, Job's comforter. Listen dear. To-morrow we'll go and see that new Gable thing at the Plaza. They say it's good. *Sure*, now, you'll be all right ?"

This came easy, a technique, you didn't even think, it was just there, came out like a clever trick, "*sure* you'll be all right ?" You could only be all right in Polar regions these days. "I'd better go up," he said.

"Wait ! Oh God, wait," she cried ; so he held her, held her whilst avalanches of noise struck downwards, held her thinking, "bloody near that."

"I must go," shouting it, breaking away from that warmth, warmth of her. "I won't be long. I'll get those people down. Should have been down hours ago. Be too casual one of these days."

He *must* go up, like on a given signal, he must go up.

He went out, calling over his shoulder, "Chin up, darling." He was gone.

He switched on his torch ; he was shouting again, " Everybody down. All below there. Come along," shining the cone of light upwards, as into voids, " all down to the cellar," thinking of the Frazers, Mrs. Robinson, "what kind of devil is he, with his bloody music, and her there, and that poor little kid ? Silly swine, I call it mad."

Hurrying up, suddenly thoughtless, deaf, hurrying up, piercing upward voids with his torch. He reached the landing, then stopped.

" Hallo ! Somebody moving about on top. Oh, Lord ! It's that woman—that painter chap ; I'll bet they've got that picture with them. Oh hell, stop me from laughing."

He was at the Frazers' door. "Hallo, there," he called out, remembered her name. "Hallo, Emily," he called through the half-open door, switching the torch off, switching it on, at times this torch could speak, he made it speak now in series of flashes. " Hallo, there ! Better get down. They've been over some time," then softer, " Hallo. *There* you are ! You know they're over, yes, heavy stuff and plenty, all over the place." Looking at her, she was in the doorway now, what he thought was her, he hated to switch this light upwards into her face, it would only frighten her. " You'd better get Mr. Frazer down, too," he said, earnest, appealing, " for heaven's sake do hurry, Mrs. Frazer. I mean Em—— where's Mr. Frazer ? "

"This won't shut," Emily said, like a sentinel to its post, her hand went to this door knob. "I wish it would shut, but it *won't*——"

Not remembering, clean forgotten. Shut !

"What shut ?" he asked, "what ?" and he switched on the torch. "Oh, I told you I'd get that door fixed to-morrow," emphatic, "now didn't I, Mrs. Frazer ?" Looking straight at her, "Where is Mr. Frazer ?" He wanted to swear, bravely held back the words, "Come on, now, I'll help you down, where *is* he ?" looking at her tired eyes ; he lowered his torch.

"He's just having tea, Mr. Jones, we'll be down after tea. We'll be all right, I'm sure we will. Mr. Frazer thinks any sort of hurry is useless these days."

"Come on, I'm responsible for *everybody* here," anger rising against this slowness, against this diversion, against nonsense, "hang the blasted door, come on."

"Mr. Jones," Emily said, "I'm surprised. We are quite able to take care of ourselves ; we shall come down when my husband has finished his tea. You are very kind, very very kind, and thoughtful, too. But half the evening we have been worried. You ought to go higher up, there's a little baby crying there, sometimes it doesn't of course, and you hear that music. Mr. Frazer hears it too, sort of jungle music ; my husband is an authority on jungle music, Mr. Jones."

She turned her back on him, she went in, she left him standing there. He went upstairs.

"And how that bloody sailor got in there is a complete mystery to me. I hope Gwen's all right, why on earth Mrs.

Robinson didn't bring the baby down as soon as it started, only God in this moment knows. I hope Gwen's comfy ; anyhow, I'll go up, I'll kick that sodden door right in, it's suicide.'' Throwing the cone of light upwards again, ''Hallo, I don't hear the rain any more ; have to get that hole seen to to-morrow, same time as the Frazers' door, the way that fellow laughs up there ; I'll get their stinking old door fixed first thing to-morrow morning, some people *do* worry, I must say. I expect Gwen's all right, *really*.'' Suddenly shouting again, ''Hey, hey, there, get down below, don't you know they're dropping stuff. I'm responsible for everybody in this house, every bloody body.'' It was no good, you couldn't hold back what you felt, *all* the time, enraged that nothing save echoes were coming back to him, of his own voice, falling from voids.

''Blast you,'' he said ; he began kicking at the Robinsons' door. ''I'd like to kick it in altogether,'' to himself ; shouting, ''Everybody out there ?'' Then he ceased kicking. He waited. That door would open, music cease, that child would cry. This would be normal. He waited, switching off his torch. He heard a fire-engine drive past, a lorry revving up, somebody shouting, ''Jackie, put that light out.'' Then nothing except music was in his ears. After a while this stopped, perhaps they had heard him after all. Switched off—''battery's run down,'' you thought this, effortless, thought it instantly, it was really clever.

''That's it, it's run down ; damned good job, I think,'' still standing patiently, waiting for the door to open, wondering how long the patience might last. He wondered, from there to hope, from there to child's cry, he hung on this.

''I hope it cries. I'll smash this damned thing in for them,'' kicking it again.

Everything was quiet whilst he waited, then above he heard feet moving, listened.

''Wait,'' a frantic cry.

''Yes, I'm waiting,'' words struggling up, ''yes, dear. God ! Do hurry.''

"It's caught—caught, the torch, Lena ; the torch, oh dear, the torch."

"I forgot it," Lena said.

" It's caught somewhere, can't you do something ?"

"A moment, be patient, *please* be patient, it's a heav—it's a weig——"

"Careful," admonishing.

"I am," sighed out.

"Don't fall, careful ; oh God, don't drop it, Lena."

"All right, I've got it, it's stuck fast ; it's caught some-where, these banisters. I'll try to get it out, pull—pull back towards you, will you pull," all in one breath, "pull now—*hard.*"

"I'm pulling, Lena."

"Good heck ! Fancy that," Richard said, "why, I forgot all about those two on the fifth floor. But why in heaven they will *bring—that—bloody—tearing—thing* everywhere they go, I don't know, I just don't know," and as though bereft, " I don't KNOW."

He hurled himself against the Robinsons' door, and as the knob on the other side had been turned, he fell inwards, flat into the room.

. . . .

The wireless was off, the child could not cry, it was feeding, behind a curtain, flimsy red. The blue man and the sailor were seated in chairs opposite each other, a blue arm half round his Philco, he could never leave this, he loved it. They had been talking, in low voices, under the music roar, talking a mumble-jumble, they could not understand each other. But now when Mr. Jones fell in they were at once laughing, and always Mr. Robinson could laugh louder than this sailor. You knew he could laugh, whole reservoirs of it behind his smiling face, dead white against blue clothes. About thirty, sandy-haired, and balding, two prominent teeth, they might be dams to this reservoir, very big teeth, a small chin, thin hands, fingers that danced on his knees, danced anywhere they might happen to be, never would be still.

"Hallo, there," the sailor said.

"Hell—LO," Robinson said, "you come right in and have a drink.'''

Mr. Jones got up. "You better all get below," he said curtly, "get below quick. Get that child down, too. And your wife. No messing about, one of these days you'll get that bloody thing smashed up for you," pointing at the wireless set, "going most of the night."

"Hallo, there," the sailor said, "goddam you look funny, come'n have one," and turning to Mr. Robinson, "*you*—this time—goddam it, yes."

"I told you I never drank," the airman said, and he was still laughing.

"I'll have a drink time enough," Richard said, looking at the blue man—the big teeth seemed to be champing their way through the now ecstatic smile. "Where's your wife and child ?" he said.

He stood just inside the door, one gloved hand on his hip, the other hung listlessly, fingers feverishly pulling off threads that weren't there, "hurry up." He felt strong standing there, just inside the door, "you don't want a bomb on you do you ?" his mind searching for words, something better to say, something to shatter that smile, choke the laughter in its offing, smash the inane stare, "been drinking half the night——"

"I told you—I never drink," the blue man said.

He didn't drink, but he could laugh. "On a leave," Richard thought, and he had a good ship-mate, too, by the look of it, looking from airman to sailor, sprawled in his chair, the face had a timeless, bovine look.

"Lil—i," the blue man called.

Then he stood up, turned the wireless on, his hand could shake atmospherics by the ship-load out of the Philco, calling above the noises, "Li—l, Li—ill," calling louder as he manipulated the switches, "Lil—ll, gentleman to see you, Mr. Jones, name Jones."

"Come'n," the sailor cried, staggering from his chair, "come'n, you're just being stubborn, sure. Come'n," leaning heavily over the table, a paw reaching for a green bottle.

"Look-out ! " the blue man said, but it was all right, he had the bottle safe, he was advancing with the gin, "now come'n have one, Mr. Jones. Hell's fire, you look so *bloody* excited," hand pushing a glass towards Richard's mouth, the other arm half-way round his back, a comforting attitude, "come'n. Don't be so goddam stubborn now."

Richard spat in the gin. "Go to hell," he said. He was thinking of Gwen. The wireless shrieked.

"There she is ! Got her ! Hell, this stuff *gets* you, gets right under your bloody old skin. Eh, sailor-man ? "

"Sure, it makes you sad," the sailor said.

"Li—ill," the airman called, louder above the tempest of sound, "gentleman to see you, says his name is Jones," half turning from the set, never releasing his hold on "volume control," he couldn't do that, like letting go on a miracle, Bolivia was a miracle, getting it. "Li—ill ! Li—ll ! " above the uproar, a little screech from his mouth, "hey, Li—l, for Christ's sake hurry up, will you ? " looking towards Mr. Jones, then at the sailor, and he was laughing again, laughing at Mr. Jones's nose being tweaked, caught between two strong sailor fingers. " You're just too goddam stubborn sure," the sailor was saying, looking from Mr. Jones to the gin, the spit in it. " Just too stubborn, eh ?"

She came out, child half over her shoulder. This was the blue man's wife.

The child hanging over, a hand clutching a silk shawl, gay golden colour. " What *dar*ling ? " she said.

" Nothing ducks, 'cept that," laughing, "nothing 'cept that. Wants to see you."

She laughed, this could be contagious. "Oh, darling, do look," she said.

"I am," the blue man said, "he looks bloody funny," floods of laughter. "Fed it ?" he said, not thinking of "it." "He wants you to take it down, wants *you* to go down, too. To the cellar, ducks. Wants to go down, darling ? Those effing bastards are over again, you know, how my finger itches. Want to go, ducks ? '' and not quite certain about it even yet. ''Fed it ?''

''I'm all right, darling,'' she said, out of a too red mouth, a thin line of mouth, this could zip open and shut, it had the machine touch, like his.

''Splendid, Excellent.''

''Exe—bloody—lent,'' the sailor chorused, pulling Mr. Jones's nose, who did not feel this, nor see them, together grouped, laughing at him, did not hear them, only thinking of Gwen, below, far below, where it was dark.

He had come up, shining a torch, shining it up to what looked like voids, where your voice could echo, like a cry in Polar regions.

''Asleep,'' the blue man said, jerking a finger at ''it,'' half hung over her shoulder making froth bubbles on a silk shawl. ''You *have* fed it ?'' voice rising, climbing over Bolivian wails, ''you have fed it ?'' like a horse, a dog, you had to feed these. He made a mad dive at ''volume control,'' they were all in Bolivia now, he turned it till he could go no further. You always felt like that when *they* were over.

He went up to her, always laughing, the reservoir was open, this could not be closed again for some time, long arms round her, dancing fingers on her shoulders, dancing, they must get somewhere. Frantic, they must search out, find a place where they could be cool, would stop convulsing, over-throwing the perpetual itch. An itch you liked in a way, an itch the sailor knew, an itch you talked about, hearing of for two hours, out of a hot mouth. He knew this itch now, something new, a change from ice.

'' Let's have a dance, shall we ?'' he said, as though the itch had worked downwards, infusoria to his legs. ''Come on, never mind the bastards overhead. Don't you know I'm on a leave ?'' clapping hands in her face, ''don't you know that, ducksie ?''

''Of course, darling, I *know*——'' out of her thin mouth, out of her cow-like face, some cows had a pretty look.

''Darling, I think you've had enough music for to-night, really, darling. I'll go down to the cellar. I think it's getting a bit too strenuous overhead, it sounds like that to me, I'll go down, I think," mouth wider, pearly teeth showing; "I'll go down with her."

"Fed it ? " he said.

" Of course, darling."

"Christy ! Look at Mr. Jones." he shouted, "just look," floods of laughter would come up.

"It *is* funny," she said, "and yet it isn't ; I mean, well, you know what I mean——"

" Of course, ducksie."

She laughed, they all laughed, it was funny, it made you laugh. He did not look funny. So serious, even with his nose being tweaked. She had a feeling that "her" was slipping over, perhaps a little too far, like a shawl slipping, a feeling your garter had loosened ; she raised a hand with five bloody tips on it, she dug at what "it" wore, something long, something white, she pulled it back. "Hallo, podgy wodgy," she said. The other hand came behind "her" back, then both hands were gripping "her," holding the child up, high, higher, looking up at it, a round face, violently red, all blood, two wide glass-like eyes. He saw.

"Blow ! I say, ducksie, you've—I mean—she's had too much, got wind," caught and held by the glass eyes, in the podgy face, "podgy" was her name by proxy christening.

"Do de do, da de dah !" she sang, raising the child up and down, and higher again, "do de dah, da de do," to the music's rhythm, it could be infectious, she was often lost in wonder at the Philco, the miracle set, never would work until he got a leave, he certainly knew a wireless when he saw one.

"Do de dah de do de dah," she sang. What a set it was, the child moving to a Bolivian rhythm.

You could tell a good set, but you *would*, for even machines could be friends, recognize each other in a room.

"I'd better go down, darling, they *are* rather close," Mrs. Robinson said. "Yes, I'd better go," telling herself, "yes yes, yes yes," this forced up decision, "I'd better go, darling, they *are* close, aren't they ?"

"Silly ! The bastards have been over hours, silly—ducks,"

and then, his voice was almost tender, as though he had thought of "it," seen "it," and the genders had changed, warmth for "it" had stolen in somehow, perhaps behind the Bolivian music. As suddenly forgetting this, "Oh, lordy lord, look, it's growing," pointing at Mr. Jones, whose nose could be pulled by a man who liked his *stuff*, name of Jones.

"Darling," Mrs. Robinson said, mouth at blue man's mouth. "It" again half-way over her shoulder.

You had "it," and there it was. There it was over your shoulder. And you had *him*, as well, home on a leave. This was an extension on wonder. You were thrilled. You had him home on leave. The accident over the shoulder was just one of those things that happened, like getting a letter, or counting your change. This was reason in her. You fed "it," you would take it down with you to the cellar.

"They are getting rather hot, darling. I wonder how long they've been over. I'll go right away. Please get me my coat, I wish you'd come, dear, I can't sit there by myself," thinking of the stairs, the stone steps, the mouse smell.

She'd take it down there with her. It would cry, but there was always something handy to stick in its mouth, you could do this in the dark cellar and there would be no fuss, not like being behind a curtain ; she still wondered why he could let a perfect stranger into their flat. It would sleep later on. It always slept when the music was turned off, she didn't like this music *all* the time, but he did, and she loved him, he was a dear of a man, a dear. They *would* come over when he had his leave.

He wrapped a coat round her shoulders. "Watch it doesn't get cold."

"I'll watch she doesn't catch cold, darling."

" We'll all go," he shouted, laughing, "let's all go down. O.K. Let's go." Mr. Robinson and his wife linked arms.

"Christy ! He does look funny," the blue man said, "you coming down, sailor-man ? We're all going to sit in the cellar with the mouses ; coming ? "

They both looked across at Mr. Jones, at this sailor, but the child hanging over a shoulder could only look at a Philco, out of glassy eyes. Mrs. Robinson had been quixotically maternal behind the red curtain, it would carry much wind into the cellar. The glassy eyes went on staring at the wireless set, Bolivia was still triumphant, the blue man had forgotten to turn it off. They stood, they laughed at Mr. Jones.

Richard said, in a quiet voice you could not hear against the music flood, "Are you finished pulling, sailor?" and the sailor heard this ; he had sharp ears, as well as the hawk's eye of his profession.

"You're so goddam stubborn," the sailor said, "people like a bit of fun, even if those buggers *are* over. In a minute," he said, almost confiding, "in a minute I'll let go."

"Bastard !" Richard said, and the sailor staggered halfway back into the room, reeled from a fist that had had all of Gwen behind it. He had thought of her as he struck out. Then he said quietly, " You forgot your manners."

"I say ! What the merry hell ?" the blue man protesting, his voice encompassed nearly two octaves in a sort of screech, he seemed to have two voices, a hollow English baritone, a bleating Italian tenor, you knew he would croon well. "I say, you can't bloody-well, stinking-well do that, you know."

He let go his hold on Mrs. Robinson, he even forgot Bolivia, he dashed across the room. "Get out," he said, "who the devil are you ? " even the swears were proprietary, "knocking my bloody friend down, who the hell are you, anyhow ?"

Yes, who was he ? With his tin helmet, a bowler hat originally, changed by magic overnight, a bowler-hatted man, *really*. " You get out of here."

He stamped a foot encased in patent leather, gorgeously shining, you knew the effeminate screech would be under way again. He was right up, almost on top of Richard, who thought of nothing except Gwen, felt nothing except that warmth he always hated to get away from. He could only think of that dark cellar now.

"Christy ! Go on ! Before I throw you out," the blue man said, so this remark made Mrs. Robinson say, "Yes, please *do* go." Who was *he*, anyhow, coming in like that, without even knocking, the idea, barging in, interfering, spoiling everything, making her blue man angry, her lovey-dovey, and then she, too, went up to Mr. Jones, she threw an arm round Mr. Robinson, whilst "it" over her shoulder was suddenly rude, but Bolivian music swallowed this up, it went unheard.

"*Darling*," she said, pinching his arm, "send him away."

"I am," he said, ignoring the pinch, "you get to the devil out, mister."

"If you are in the cellar, I'll be there too," Richard said. He turned away, he went out.

They heard him start off down the stairs, but there was a sudden halt. The blue man shut the door.

"I like his damned cheek. For two pins I'd have thrown him out," looking down at her, all eyes of a sudden, the ecstatic smile came back, and her face seemed to be floating up to him, flooded with adoration. She was like that with her blue man. She hadn't a pretty cow face for nothing.

"*Darling*," she said again, up to his smile.

"Hey, sailor ! You all right ?"

He went over and helped pick Mr. Johns up. He was stood up now, but he held on to him ; he might fall again, sailor's legs in cities were like that. He looked at Mr. Johns, at a ruby nose outshining red-stained chin, a soiled shirt neck.

"Let's get down below," Mr. Robinson said, leaving Johns on an even keel ; he went to the table, he switched off, he picked up the Philco, this would go with him to the cellar, it would get Bolivia again, it might amuse the mice, the bright-eyed rat that came visiting sometimes from a nest snug between two dustbins.

"Well, is everything ready now ?" the blue man said, he looked over at the sailor, rather pityingly, he said quickly, "Bring your gin, I know you can't survive without that sort of thing," and the laughter was rolling out again, he filled the room with it, you could never really trace it to source, it had epidemic proportions, would be doctor-confounding.

She laughed, the sailor laughed, she thought how witty "darling" was, watching Mr. Johns put the gin bottle in his pocket.

"Sure ! I'm fine," the sailor said.

"This is going to be an all-night do," the blue man said. "I wish I was up there, I'd let those effing bastards know a thing or two," again laughter, but this was different in tone. "Let's get out," he said quickly, decision reached, "let's all go below."

"Yes, *darling*, but hadn't you better bring the thermos, too ?"

"Yes, ducks, but I can't manage that *and* the set, can I ? "

"No, *darling, he'll* bring it. I'll go and get it."

She went and got the ever-ready thermos from behind the red curtain, the coffee-filled flask, this was always on tap. She handed it to the sailor.

"Carry it down for me, Mr. ——er," smiling at the sailor.

"Johns," he said, "Johns the name is," showing green teeth.

"All right, Mr. Johns," Mrs. Robinson said.

"Babby looks ill," the sailor said.

"Oh podgy-wodgy," she said, bringing its face again level with her own, "Da da de do de dah," kissing it, she seemed to suck at podgy rather than kiss her, "do de da de doh."

The blue man was at the door. "Come on," he said, a fury in him, he had heard a noise, a deafening explosion, crackling sounds, he thought, "we better join the mouses quick."

They went out, the blue man closed the door. "Torch ! Shine a bloody light."

This shone as from nowhere, instant, one of those miracles, like getting Bolivia. This shone downwards from Mrs. Robinson's hand, shone towards a flight of stairs. She always carried a torch, she had a zip pocket, you could fish it out any time, and the darkness lately wasn't of the ordinary kind, you had to have a torch handy for everything these nights.

"Move," the blue man said.

"We are, *darling*. Aren't we, Mr. Johns ?"

"Sure ! We're moving all right. Christ ! I think you're fine, Mrs. Robinson," he said.

.   .   .   .

Mr. Frazer, shaved, a cut here and there, said, ''Aren't you having a cup of tea, Emily ?''

He was out of his dressing-gown, his grey hair was parted in the middle, he wore a rubber collar, slightly yellow at the edges, a pale red tie, he never bothered much about colours, the main thing was to get a tie knotted without too much doddering. He knew he doddered, was old, all of a sudden old, surprise with the vice in it.

''Aren't you—do you mind, dear ?'' looking at his wife, ''come, dear,'' half-rising from his chair, then suddenly sitting down again, seeing Emily moving, she was going to sit down after all.

''I wish you wouldn't stand by that door all the time, dear,'' he said.

''Mr. Jones told me he would get it fixed, dear,'' Emily said. She came over and sat by him.

''Did he ? '' Mr. Frazer said, and then he concentrated on tea-drinking, why talk any more about the door ? He knew it would never be fixed now.

He knew, who had lived much longer than Mr. Jones. It had been a blow, waking up in the night and finding it half-open, something had got in, too, he realized that, a gust of wind, something *had* happened. He looked across at Emily.

''You know I couldn't sleep with that row upstairs, I gave it up,'' he went on, reaching across the table for the tea-pot, and this always made Emily feel a little afraid. Once Mr. Frazer would always use his right hand to get this pot, now he used his left. And there were other things that made her afraid. Putting things back on shelves, drawing curtains, filling a kettle, turning a tap, you noticed these little things, why suddenly did he use his left hand ? All his life he had been a right-handed man, always the left was clumsy, dropping things. Her eyes were riveted on her husband's right hand.

''I wish you'd try not to be so odd, dear,'' she said, thinking back, remembering his trying to shave with his left hand. She would watch it motionless, whilst the other moved, it seemed to be hiding itself, it drew back. She remembered, too, how, when he first tried to close the door, he had used the alien hand, in the most natural way, as though all his life he had been a left-handed man. Even the discovery that they had slept all night with this door open, blown open by a *force*, even this paled when the left hand usurped, the right was useless.

She still thought it was a funny idea for her to have, yet its funniness was not something she could laugh at. She could still think that overnight the right hand had become suddenly ashamed of all that it had done.

He spilt tea into his saucer, the pot shaking in the odd hand. She got up.

"Oh, do let me do it, dear," she protested, taking the teapot from him. She filled his cup, sugared and milked it for him.

"It was all right, dear," Mr. Frazer said, "it was quite all right," and after a slight pause, "I can still hear those people overhead."

"Yes. Those people are still overhead," Emily said, putting fresh tea into her cup. "Mr. Jones wants us to go down to the cellar right away, but I said you were finishing your tea, and he seemed satisfied with that, and went away."

She often thought of Richard in terms of direct authority, like a stationmaster, like a prison-warder, a policeman. She could remember a hale and hearty Mr. Jones, travelling in chemicals, before the great convulsion began, always happy, and, like the Welsh will, holding on hard to a Welshness which was the soft yell in his singing voice. She used to love to hear him singing, how happy he was then, filling all the house with this golden stuff, brought to a great city from a little country of soft valleys, of little people, of golden mouths. She often thought of him in his bowler hat, and the blue serge suit, a perennial trust in blue serge, the double-breasted coat, the trousers peg-topped as near as peg-topped can be. And now he was just a little different.

"I wonder how long those people have been over, dear," Mr. Frazer said ; he was getting up, he was pushing away his chair with his left hand. "I wonder."

Emily laughed. "I thought you said you hadn't slept," she said, getting up, too, "those people have been overhead hours now. I heard Mr. Jones say that it would be an all-night affair," saying this to Mr. Frazer, as though there would be dancing till 3 a.m., refreshments afterwards.

" An all-night affair," she said. " That's what Mr. Jones thinks, dear."

He nodded at her, doddered away from the table, he went to the fire, sat down by it. He had forgotten the urge behind Mr. Jones's shouting voice, behind Emily's.

"Do hurry, dear," she said, seeing him making himself comfortable. He had completely forgotten those people, left-handedly he lit a pipe.

"I've got everything ready," Emily said, who had not forgotten those people and the journey to the cellar that must be made.

They had gone away, all had been quiet. Now they were back again. Mr. Frazer always referred to the high drones as inklings that those people were over again, and Emily would say, "those people are horrid, dear."

They had heard them referred to as Germans, Nazis, swines, and bastards, but somehow everything could be covered by two words, "those people."

"I'll wind the clock, dear," Mr. Frazer said, getting up at once to do it, but she was there before him. She took the clock, she wound it. He could do anything with the left hand, but it could not wind this clock.

"All right, dear," she said, "it's quite all right. It's done," full of assurances, "you had better get your ulster, dear, and the scarves. *I'll* bring the blanket, and don't worry too much, they won't stay over long, at least I don't think they will."

She turned off the gas-fire, she put on her heavy brown coat, wrapped two scarves about her neck, she dropped a half-flask of brandy into Mr. Frazer's capacious pocket, the ulster was like a handy bag, and it had a magpie habit of collecting things, too. He didn't notice the bottle being put in. He was absent-minded, he was doddering about the room. He put an empty kettle on a gas-jet, which Emily at once retrieved, banging it down on the stone flags, turning off the jet of flame.

"Are you ready, now, dear?" she said.

He looked up at her, he hesitated, he was ready, but somehow he couldn't say so. He was thinking hard. Getting ready, going to the cellar, it all came back to him, panorama flashes reeling past tired eyes, that sometimes watered. Thinking of the door. That was the thing that troubled. She was calm now, calm talking, calm making tea, but when they were going out he knew she would stop dead, hold on to the door knob. She would hate to go to the cellar and leave it open, the door dominated, overwhelmed.

She was looking at him, the folded blanket over her arm. "Ready now, dear?"

He shook violently, a long swishing sound went past the window of their room.

"Are you ready?" she said again. "I can hear Mr. Jones. He's shouting up again," thinking in stationmaster terms, Mr. Jones might be shouting, "Last train going, definitely the last train that will ever go. This *is* the last train."

"I'm ready," Mr. Frazer said, slowing moving out of the room, she following. And outside they stopped. He knew this would happen, he caught hold of Emily's hand, he held it.

"If only it would shut," she said.

"I know, dear," stuttering, thinking how everything that could be said about it had already been said. "I know, dear."

Nothing else you could say. There it was. Door of a room that held all their lives, together lived, all in this room. There had never been any other place. All had been builded here since his retirement from work, and weekly, as regular as clockwork, his Government pension for services rendered had come through that letter-box, O.H.M.S. There it was. Open.

"Come, dear," appealing, sorry for Emily, she felt about this door keenly, so did he, but he had to try and be practical, he had to try and be normal, even though he doddered, and she hated his left hand. He essayed a smile.

"Come, dear, I'm sure Mr. Jones will get it fixed."

You had to force the words out, you had to say something. There it was, the hand on the door, and the same expression on Emily's face. She might be on the verge of a great journey;

he often thought how odd it was that she should think him a changed man, women were illogical creatures, surely it was Emily who had changed. A journey downstairs to a cellar, where you sat in the dark with others, where you didn't really fit in, you were old, of a time when things were normal and doors closed in a natural way, as they were meant to do. Sitting in a cellar where people talked, but you didn't understand very much, the tempo of everything was new, even the language they used was new, you didn't seem to have the right key to it.

"Oh dear, dear ! Do come," he said, "*do* come," hopelessness stealing over him, now that he felt that vice-like grip on the knob. And, endeavouring to be as calm as possible, "come along now, dear, it's only a few flights down. Do come, Emily ! "

There it was. You had to appeal, you had always to conserve your energy, energy in store to share out with the remaining days you had, to keep the rhythm of days equal.

"Mr. Jones will get it fixed, dear."

But Emily, who might be on a journey across an endless Sahara, said quietly, as though coolness had come to thoughts, "I don't feel safe with it open, dear," hanging on.

How could he loose that grip on the knob ?

A laughter peal came from upstairs, he looked in that direction, it was dark. Then he saw a light flashing in and out. He heard feet on the stairs, people talking, more laughter. His hand was on her hand. Emily let go, not violently, it just lifted itself away from the knob, it was free.

"There !" Mr. Frazer said, he was relieved, and now he knew how it had happened. She had heard laughter from above, he was sure it was this that had loosened her hold on the door.

"Come now, dear," moving down, slow, careful ; they had no torch, they didn't much bother about them, they never went out any place, they never wanted torches. They went down, step by slow step, hand in each other's hand, they had left the room where all their life was, left the door half-open, the room leased to something that had got in, it was still there, it had blown in through the open door, whilst they slept, leased it whilst they went downwards towards the cellar.

"Oh Christ ! Lena ! Can't you move it now ? Try again, dear."

"Oh !" Emily jumped. "What's that, dear ?"

"I don't know," Mr. Frazer said, "somebody talking upstairs, I think," and then he was calling down in his cracked voice, "Are you there, Mr. Jones ? Are you there ?" and then Emily called in the same way, her voice as thin and cracked as his, calling, "Oh, Mr. Jones, Mr. Jones," for he was a stationmaster again, and the last train going. The platform was long and dark, you had to grope your way, he would see them safely along the platform, he would see them comfortable in the waiting-room. You waited there in the dark, you had a part to play.

You didn't know what part you would take in this play, it *was* like a play. You just sat and waited there, listening to people talking, the other actors and none of them knew the name of this play, what their parts would be. They just waited, play unknown, actors unseen.

"Are you there, Mr. Jones ?"

"Hallo, there," Richard said, laughing upwards, a velvet laugh, the legacy from valleys, the golden touch. "Hallo, Mrs. Frazer, Mr. Frazer come, too ?"

"We're here, we're all right, Mr. Jones," the old man said, a fatherly tone in his voice, like Richard was their son. "We're coming," and quickly interrupted by Emily, who said, "the door still won't shut, Mr. Jones. Are you going to get it fixed, Mr. Jones ?"

"To-morrow," Richard said, "here we are !" switching the light on, they blinked, they stood still, they were on the verge of abysses.

"Half a mo," Mr. Jones said.

He took her hand, took his, he led them down, slowly, carefully, he was quite calm, as though all the pressures of these hours had been nothing, purely imagined ones.

"Careful ! And don't worry about the door. I will see to

it, that it's fixed to-morrow. Careful ! Now another flight, careful ! You'll find Mrs. Jones down there, oh, and there's a young woman, too, rather drunk, but she won't worry you. In fact, she's fast asleep,'' saying all this at speed, indifferent to outside tumult, the noises, what hung high in sky with the hawk's eye, to what sounded like hell's engines.

"There we are ! Now slowly down these steps, and don't *worry, don't* worry,'' his voice earnest, appealing, his voice seeming to say, "catch hold, make a strong grip, you are safe, you have a sure hold on all normality, which I am, now, always was, and will be, even touching Gwen's warmth, even away from it, listening to cries in the Polar regions, and not to the beat of her heart, which circles mine and fastens there, throb by throb.

"Easy ! Watch that stair ! It's smashed,'' he said.

" Thank you, Mr. Jones, thank you,'' Emily said.

"Thank you, Mr. Jones, thanks,'' Mr. Frazer said, going down, hand in Mr. Jones's hand, he might be his own son.

"Three more steps,'' Richard said. "Careful again.''

"Thank you, Mr. Jones,'' Emily said.

"Here we are, we're on the bottom step now,'' Richard said, calling, "Gwen, Gwe—n. You all right, darling ?'' and softly back, "I'm all right, dear, are you coming in ?''

"Yes. Just bringing in Mr. and Mrs. Frazer, will you move up a bit, make room for them ? '' and as though to himself, "I wonder whether we oughtn't to have some kind of light down here now,'' wondering whether the old wooden partition would effectively screen the entrance way. It was a job in the dark at any time, you never knew when your hand would grip a rusty nail, all nails, really.

"I wonder ?''

"All right. Here we are ! Mind your head, Mr. Frazer, Mrs. Frazer,'' laughing, "this is a bit of a caution, isn't it. Talk about a cave. Oh well, easy now, there, you're in at last. That's good. That's splendid.''

"Oh dear,'' Emily said, lost in a vastness, even a darkness eight feet by five could give a feeling of endlessness, of nothing but height, depths. She stumbled, cried out, "Oh, what's that ?"

"Ssh !" Richard said, "it's only that young woman. By the lord Harry she *does* snore, doesn't she ? Here we are again. Now sit down, Mr. Frazer, that's it. Yes, everything's all right, the seat's right behind you, take his hand, Gwen."

"Yes, dear."

"Now, Mrs. Frazer. That's it. There you are. All fine and comfy," leaning over them, reaching to where Gwen was, gripping her arm, "I'll light the light, dear ; are you all right, darling, *sure* ?" and the voice lowered to whispers, the mouth to her ear, a sort of language the Frazers didn't comprehend, whispering fiercely, "Yes. Three! Outside. Good Lord ! You heard, didn't you ? *must* have heard that explosion, yes, it's gone. Reilly's place blazing. Are you all right ?" saying this fiercely, meaning this, whilst the whole cellar shook, a giant amok, vibrations, lifting it up, lifting it down. He gripped her hands.

He must sit down, he must hold her. He knew what this was, the terror language. Think of Gwen who knew the idiom, all the words of this language, think of her, not the Frazers, their labels said "Lost."

"Hold on to me, dear," half-crying at her ear, at her mouth, "O, Jesus, hold me, Gwen, hold on to me," the emanation there, the weight coming, downwards with the speed of light, from an iron mouth, frenzy's vomit.

Crushing her to him, crushing hard. "Ah, Jesus ! Wait ! Ah, Jesus ! Be with us !" and loudly, as now it no longer mattered about two who were old, about a drunken piece, loudly, "Wait, wait, Jesus !" hand in her hand, the other feeling forehead's sweat, Jesus large in his mind. Long ago he had sung Jesus softly in a child's dress, he had touched a Jerusalem wonder in a child's room, at a child's desk, "wait," as though this man were there, and he were waiting, "Oh, Jesus. Gwen—Gwen," one arm round her, free hand still touching a hot forehead. If He were here, the wonder touched in crib at Llanganoch in the long ago, He would touch this sweat, He would know what sweat was. And louder, "Gwen, oh darling, Gwen," herself crushed, lost in his arms, her hair on his face, on his half-laughing, half-crying face.

"Pray, dear," Emily said, "pray."

"Yes, pray, son," Mr. Frazer said, "*do* pray," and then no more was said, or heard, and the drunken snore lost, and Gwen falling, somewhere, "Oh, God ! Gwen !"

"Are you all right, dear ?" Emily said, holding Mr. Frazer's hand, and he said, "Oh ——" and he said, "Yes ——" his heart heaving, it might leap into the throat, because they were over, those people, because something had fallen near, had exploded. They were clung together, they were in the wilderness.

"Pray, Emily, pray for Mr. Jones."

"I am, dear. I am praying for Mr. Jones. I always liked poor Mr. Jones."

"Gwe—n."

"What, dear ?"

"Oh ——" Richard said, "oh—something happened."

"It's all right, Richard," Gwen said, "it's all right now. It seemed so near. How hot you are."

"Am I ?" lifting himself up, "heavens, Gwen, we're on the floor."

"So we are," Gwen said, feeling cold stone, touch of grey mould, near a mouse smell, "so we are," began to laugh softly, as though his laughter was secret, severely rationed, was crying as softly, so he laughed, he held her tight.

"Are *you* all right, son ?" Mr. Frazer said, as if all the time he had been on a calm sea, sailing serene, "are you all right, son ?" for Richard was now son, flesh and blood son to him.

"I'm all right, Mr. Frazer, are you ?" Richard said, out of a dry mouth.

"We're all right," Emily said, returned from the same calm sea, soldier's wind there, "we're all right, Mr. Jones."

"That's good," Mr. Jones said, not knowing his voice was quaking, "that's good. I must try and find my matches."

"You know," Mrs. Frazer said, "you know that it's begun to rain again."

"Is it ?" Richard said.

"Oh, yes," Mrs. Frazer replied.

This was glass raining, this was raining glass.

"Listen," Gwen said.

He listened. He jumped to his feet, he said, "Won't be long," he rushed out of the cellar, he banged into a dustbin on the way out, he knew what to do. Gwen was in, the Frazers were, but the others. They must get into the cellar right away. They mut get down, *now*. This was a night stretched out, stretched to the ultimate, this was *long* night, it might never end, *they* might never go.

"This is the worst yet," he said loudly as though addressing multitudes, switching on his torch. Then he stood still, he stood still and said, "Hey there !"

.   .   .   .

"What the stinking merry hell," the blue man said, "what's this, what's all this ? Come to do the bloody decorating or something," a torch shining in Clem's face, in Lena's. The sailor was behind him, Mrs. Robinson and child behind the sailor. "What the merry hell's going on here, anyhow ?"

"Oh, heavens," Mrs. Robinson said, remembering a previous night, "oh, heavens !"

"Moving house," the sailor said, "sure that's fine. I'll give you a hand."

Lena sat on a chair, Clem sat. They were resting. The canvas was stuck. He would not move, she would not leave him, never. She sat there, watching him, they were resting together. They had heard the bomb, but they had said nothing. There was nothing you could say. When you understood you said nothing. The cone of light was cruel in her eyes, in Clem's.

"Please take the light off my eyes," Lena said quietly, shading them with her hand.

"Only trying to help you, you know," the blue man said, "after all"—a sudden pause—"they were all listening."

"I say, ducks, you'd better get down below. Go on ! Yes, of course, what the merry hell, of course, take the kid down," he said, speaking slowly.   He had suddenly remembered that the child was not of the neuter gender.

"Sailor-man, please take Mrs. Robinson down to the cellar," patting the broad shoulder of Mr. Johns, looking at his wife, at "it."   "All right, ducksie, I won't be long, trust me.   Just going to help the furniture man," thought this funny, he was laughing again, he had to laugh.

You didn't expect *this*, you couldn't in all reason expect it, not with those effing bastards, those stinkers swinging a terror cradle over your city.   Sitting there, like they were lost in the dark, and what a queer-looking chap he was.   And didn't he smell.   Probably took strong vinegar draughts as soon as the effing bastards came over, perhaps he got Dutch courage out of a Midland vinegar bottle.   No accounting for tastes in this bloody, stinking, merry hell of a war, no accounting for palates.   The upsurge of thoughts set his fingers dancing again.   They danced on the stair rail, they raced each other there.   "Intelligent rat," he supposed.

Sharply, "Merry hell !   Do go on, ducks," a shriek, "Christy !   The way you look, ducks, you'd think I was forcing a sailor-man on you," he stopped, no, you wouldn't think at all.   That was it, you wouldn't think at all.

"All right, Mrs. Robinson," the sailor said, "carry the babby if you like.   Shine your torch, will you ?"

"There," she said, and it was shining downwards.   She stepped down two stairs, he followed, clod-hopping down.

Lena had stood up, she was leaning close to the wall.   She would let them pass.

"Stand up, dear," she said, and he stood, obedient, he was like her doll, now, in these moments when everything you touched trembled, as though reverberations of earthquakes were passing through this house.   And then she had to push Clem.   He, too, leaned against the wall.   He said nothing.

Mr. Robinson shone his torch after them as they went down. "Make her comfy, sailor," he called out, "I won't be long."

"Sure !   That's fine !   But don't you be too long, Mr.

Robinson,'' turning round, waving a hand, smiling up at the blue man, as though to say, ''Don't be too long, you know what sailors are.''

He carried ''babby'' in his arms, they reached the bottom stair, they were lost to view. In between laughter peals the blue man shouted after them. ''O.K.'' he said. ''Right you bloody well are, sailor.'' He turned to Clem. ''Now, what about shifting this bloody thing, eh? Where's it stuck?'' grabbing it at a corner, furiously pulling, thinking, ''What the merry hell is it, anyhow? What they want it for? Crazy. Crazy. Shifting house in the middle of a stinking raid.'' He looked at Lena. ''Hadn't you better go into the cellar—la—Mrs.—I don't know your name.''

''Are you all right?'' Lena said, looking at Clem. ''Are you all right, now?''

''I'm all right. I thought it was my head starting again but it's all right.''

''Christy! You can't stand here all the stinking night, really you can't. Just supposing you're killed, supposing they dropped one on here, now, suppose that. *Just* suppose.''

Lena was moving, she was going up, she was crushing past the blue man, she stumbled, she fell over his Philco.

He said, ''Oh, hell!'' trying to laugh, oddly enough this would not come out, ''lordy lord,\ can't you mind where you're going,'' the torch shining on her again, on his Philco. He helped her up. ''Now listen,'' he said, ''you go down and get a place in the cellar. Your husband and I will manage this thing all right, don't you worry about it,'' and with all-out confidence, ''*you'll* be all right, my wife's there.''

She turned and looked at him. She said, ''Thank you. Help me to get it clear.''

They pulled, the picture was free.

''What is it?''

''A picture.''

''Oh!—what's he going to do with it?'' shining the torch on it, he roared laughing, ''Oh——'' he said—''I see.''

Lena thought, ''He—what was *he* going to do with it,'' as

if Clem were miles away. She looked at his twitching face again. "My husband will tell you."

"Hang, why of course," he said, turning to Clem, "where the devil are you taking the thing, anyhow. Don't you know they're over, dropping stuff, hell, I wish my fingers weren't off buttons, oh, hell——"

"Into the cellar," Clem said.

"The cellar ! But the bloody, stinking cellar's nearly full already. Look here, Mrs.—I'm sure you'd better get down right away," his sharp ears recognizing an old sound, he knew this well, something crackling, a fire, somewhere near, he could smell it now. Crackling, "too bloody close."

"You get down at once," he said, holding Lena's arm, "you get down, Mrs.——" and turning to Clem, "now is there any reason on earth, on this bloody old earth, I ask you is there any reason at all why you must move the bloody thing down there ?"—he pulled up suddenly. Clem was looking at him, he could feel the eyes on his face ; he added, "I mean, well, but anyhow you can't. I mean the picture, course I thought it was bloody furniture at first, can't tell anything in this stinking dark, can you ?" insistent, "Now can you tell anything in this stinking dark ? Well—besides look at it. Too big. I think you ought to take it back, no, by God, leave it there, that's it," speaking quickly, it was like a revelation, "leave it. Get down," and he shouted at the top of his voice, "get down quick," then shouting "hell's stinking bells," and then the shower of dust came down, covering them, covering the picture.

"Christy !" the blue man said, pushing past, moving at speed downstairs, calling, "Oo—ee !" Ducksie ! There, ducks," stuttering, "hallo, hallo," laughing ceased, he was filled with dread. The light danced in front of him as he ran, the light vanished. They were in darkness again.

"Are you all right, now ?" Lena said.

She went to him. "Are you all right," thinking of the journey down, more flights, three, perhaps four, you didn't count flights in a journey ending endlessly.

"Lena."

"What ?"

She felt arms round her. " Lena ! Leave me. Go down. Please go down."

"Are you all right ?"

He said, "It's my head."

"Your head," she said, "paining again ?"

He nodded.

"All right," Lena said, "you wait here. I'll slip up for the pills. Would you like the bandage again ?" already passing him, thinking of his head, of how lately the pains had increased, believing in the pills Dr. Beacham left him, doubting them.

He sat down on the stair again, he said nothing, as though he hadn't heard a single word she'd spoken.

She was hurrying upstairs, groping her way back ; he had said nothing, and she was glad of that. She ought to have realized, ought to have known. Why hadn't she brought the pills, the vinegar bandages, always these things helped, they were the things that cooled, cooled a head that seemed to have been burning ever since she had known him. She ought really to have remembered. How foolish. After all there was so little he asked for, he was always so patient, so good at hiding things. Then she said, "Oh !" the word leaping out of her mouth, "oh——." The pressure again, the pain in the chest. She put her hand there. "And yet, it's nothing," leaning on the stair rail, "really it's nothing."

She reached the top of the stairs. Very dark up here after the brilliance of torches, but she knew the way to go, quickly, she could not stumble here. She went into the room, switched on the light. She got the pills and the cool bandages from the table by his bed, and came out again, then stopped, turned back, she went to the kitchen.

"I'd like a glass of real cool water, my mouth feels so dry," she said, turning on the tap.

.   .   .   .

"Look out, blast you !" Richard said, coming upstairs. "Not blind. are you ?" How could you be blind in a blaze

of light ? Two cones of light piercing each other, two faces
drenched with it. ?

"I say, merry hell, that was a stinker, wasn't it ? You
heard that one. Bloody close. I say, is my wife down
there ? Is she all right ? Look out, bugger you, I believe
you're deliberately blocking my way," the blue man said,
calling to black depths. "Oo——ee ! Hi ! Hi ! You
are all right, ducksie ?"

From these depths he heard a man talking. He was
relieved. This was Mr. Johns. He was talking about whisky.

"Who's stopping you ?" Richard said, "they're in the
cellar. I saw them in, you'd better join them there."

Mr. Robinson went down three stairs.

"Thanks," he said. "O.K. I didn't know whether they'd
got in before that effing bastard dropped that one."

"They're all right," Mr. Jones said.

"Christy ! I say, there's a chap up there," the blue man
said, waving an arm, "queer little bugger, really, looks like a
—well—oh hell ! He's got some huge thing there, calls
it a picture, suppose it is, I never noticed," all in a breath,
"It made me laugh, he won't let go of it. Let's go up. Come
on, the poor devil wants to get it down here."

"He always does," Mr. Jones said, "but you get into the
cellar. That's your place. With your wife and child. I'll
see to him," forcing his way past.

"Hell's stinking bells, only trying to help, Christy ! *he*
was just the same."

"You get into the bloody cellar, that's all. You've had
too much," he said, "like your sailor friend——"

"Eh ?" and then a violent protest, "but I don't drink,
lordy lord, I never touch the stuff," he burst into laughter
again, the well had not run dry.

"That's your place, anyhow. What I say goes here.
Remember that, will you ?" He was past, he went on up,
he swung round and called down, "Go ahead," began to
laugh himself, "I can assure you it's all right down here.
Quite a nice party in fact, if I may say so."

"You think you can manage that furniture then ?"

Mr. Jones made no reply, he disappeared round a bend in the staircase, he was going up the next flight. He heard Mr. Robinson go down. He felt more comfortable now. He wondered which was worst, mad drunk or mad sober. So he came to where Clem was sitting.

"There you are then," Mr. Jones said. He immediately sat down on a lower stair, shone the torch downwards. Suddenly he switched it towards the picture.

"Let me help you, Mr. Stevens," he said, "it's awkward to get round stair bends," as if he had always helped at this kind of thing, as though he had always been close to Clem, knew the touch on pictures.

"But it won't go into the cellar, I assure you, it's too big," and then he was amazed at himself. Somehow he was looking at himself, and amazement grew.

How could he be so quiet, so cool, like this, as though nothing in the wide world mattered but that this picture should go down to a dark cellar ? He could not answer that.

"It was too big last time, and it's still too big, Mr. Stevens," gripping a sleeve, wiping something off the corner of the canvas, a sort of smudge, the movement was imperceptible. He put a hand on Clem's arm. "Come on, we'll see what we can do," stood up, gripped with both hands, began to pull, lifted, "by heck, it's heavy," suddenly let it go, it made a loud resounding noise on the bare stairs. He remembered the woman. She wasn't here. " Where's Mrs. Stevens ?" he said.

"Here ! I'm here," Lena said, out of a void, she had come down noiselessly, she was looking down on two heads, two heads near to one another as if they had been exchanging confidences. He flashed his light up, half lowered it, he saw Mrs. Stevens. So her name *was* Stevens.

"Light always seems to hurt her eyes."

He was looking directly at her. "Everybody should be below, Mrs. Stevens. It's getting worse, I'll give him a hand with it."

"What ?" Lena said. "Worse ? What was ? The weather ?"

For once he stared into a vacant face. The something "worse" had been too big a question.

"But I'm dead certain it won't go into the cellar," he said, whispering the words over Clem's head, he wasn't really there, he was far away somewhere, he wasn't noticed. There was only the woman there and he was explaining to her. Clear facts and a clear situation.

"Why?" Clem said, so quietly that Mr. Jones exclaimed, "Eh, what's that?"

"Why?" again, and that was all Clem said.

Richard stepped up past him. He was close to this woman, closer than he had ever been. He whispered, "But it's no use. I assure you it won't go in. Besides the place is half full of people already. I do wish you'd go down, really I do," closer to this woman than he had ever been, as though all his life he had been close, to the white face, the strong, the hard, the almost masculine face, the austerity there.

"Do let me help you. I'll tell you what, you and he go down now, right away, I'll see to this. I'll see everything's all right, nothing will happen to it," this was a toy, a doll, a box of soldiers, these were children and he was talking to them, with the warmth of a father, with his authority. "I'll see nothing happens to it, really I will," children approaching the dark bedroom, he always assuring them, "darkness is nothing. It won't harm you."

He raised the light a little, he saw her face in shadow, a quiet face, and then he was remembering the drunken *piece*, remembered this quiet face looking at him, at Gwen, remembering her saying how she had never shouted, nor had he, and he said quickly as if the last drop of his earnestness were reached, "You take Mr. Stevens down," the light focused on Clem, seeing the flat of two hands pressed to his head, he thought, "that's right, I believe he always has headaches."

"He looks ill," he said, and again, "I'll see no harm comes to this, honestly I will. I'll take care of it. Do go down. It's very dangerous. I'm sure you understand," looking at the picture now, suddenly wondering why a child's slobber should be on one corner of it, "it's dangerous, it's—but you can hear—I mean—I'm sure——" he stopped, thinking, "no, that's wrong, that's wrong. Silly. Rubbish! I won't say it again."

"Thank you," Lena said, "you are very good, but I think we can manage. If you would just help me a little," pausing still a little uncertainty in her voice, and in a fierce whisper as she leaned over, "he won't let the picture go. He won't leave it. There's a reason, but you wouldn't understand—yet."

Absentmindedly Mr. Jones switched out the light. He didn't understand, and she said he didn't. Understand what? Not understanding each other, in this too sudden darkness, why? And he switched on his light again.

"Please let me help you," he said, and "please go down, take Mr. Stevens into the cellar," and "do go down right away, it's very dangerous, just listen to *that*," and then there was nothing more to say, nothing more. You were finished. You had emptied yourself.

"All right," he said, "can you lift your end?" as he thought furiously, "ought to have gone down. I'm the only authority here, by rights, should have done what they were told. Everybody else had obeyed his orders, why not they?"

"All right, lift——" and catching his breath, "lift—u—p."

She lifted. He said, "Mr. Stevens, move back a little."

"He's all right," Lena said. "Just round this bend, I'll manage the rest," worming her way down the stairs. "It's very good of you."

"Warden! Warden! Hallo there, warden! Hurry up. Quick. Wanted."

Mr. Jones stiffened, his grip on the canvas stronger; he said, "Oh hell."

He heard it again, "Warden! Warden!" He eased the weight down, he rested the canvas on the stair.

"Listen," he said.

"I can hear," Lena said.

He reached up, he suddenly touched her hand, he had not touched this before, it was like bridging a distance. "Listen," Mr. Jones said.

"I heard."

"Yes, but I have to go. Right away. Can you manage? I mean—oh, hell, all right, I'm coming—Sure you can manage?—Wish you'd get down there, leave the thing here—coming, coming! Look here——" words rushing out, a flood, a mere babble, "I—do go down, do go down. Leave it, leave it," and at the top of his voice, "Oh, blast and blast you again, I'm *coming*."

He turned round, he was rushing headlong down four flights of stairs.

Lena sat down. "Clem."

"Clem," she said again.

She touched his hands. "Let me put the bandage on for you. Rest a bit. Don't worry, please don't worry," thinking of four flights down, thinking of quietness here, on these stairs, island quietness, above tidal waters, "if only his head —if only he didn't get these pains."

"There!" a white coolness round his forehead. "But it's good," she thought, "yes—yes, it's good, I know it is, I know." She knew. It wasn't silly, it could not be laughed at. They didn't understand, they were kind, but they didn't really understand. "Rest a bit," she said, "we'll manage. You still want to go down."

"Yes," he said.

"These pains in his head seem to have got worse lately,' she thought. "It's these raids."

"Mr. Jones was kind," she said.

"Yes."

"*And* his wife."

"Yes."

"You still don't think it's worth your while contacting Renton again?"

"No."

"Not even Cruickshank," she said.

"I said NO."

"All right then. We shan't bother."

Suddenly she exclaimed, "Oh Lord! How odd."

"What?"

"Oh, nothing."

She sat down again.

"How very odd." She hadn't noticed it. She said, "Oh." This confirmed. Why hadn't she noticed it before. Words echoed back to you when you spoke. So, working slowly, from bottom upwards, you reached the heights, and it was shell.

"Shell," she thought, "hollow."

How high the words climbed, up to the roof, then heavily fell, like swooping birds. Five floors up and it was shell. How odd. You only noticed it now, after all that long time.

"But he knew from the beginning, of course he'd know."

"That airman likes his music," she said, casual, there seemed no need to hurry.

"Yes," Clem said.

Words seemed at a premium, you had to be sparing, cautious, "yes."

"Let's go down," she said.

"All right."

They started off again.

CHAPTER V

"Listen to the mouses," the blue man said.

But they were not listening to mouses, only to a stillness suddenly come to this cellar. Once it had rocked, they had fallen in a heap together, you did not know whom you clutched, the candle had gone out. Now there was this stillness, you heard yourself breathe.

"Listen to the bloody mouses," the blue man said.

The mouses were three floors up, carpet-slippered, coming slowly down, they were carrying a world between them. They made creaking noises as they descended. To Mr. Robinson they were mice.

The cellar was oblong in shape, and along each damp shining wall stretched a wooden bench. The candle stood

in a tin, clumsily fastened to the wall. It continually spluttered, it always fought the damp, it cast shadows on the
concrete floor where Celia lay, in deep sleep, sometimes she
had cried out in her sleep, but she was now far beyond green
jungle, she was in a calm sea. Near the entrance, heavily
snoring, lay Mr. Johns, his backside to the world. He, too,
was in deep sea, he was becalmed. To his left stood the
dustbins, three of them. On the bench facing these sat the
blue man, his wife and child. He had not noticed that she
was sitting on the concrete floor, easily, silently she had slipped
down from the wooden bench, but she had not noticed the
coldness there. The child lay flat across her lap, it sucked
loudly at damp air. Next to the blue man was his Philco,
always a hand rested on this. Sometimes his fingers drummed
on it. From time to time he had got up and dashed to the
door, stuck his head out and looked around, leaning over the
sailor. He would then return with a report, he was generous
with reports. He would say, "lull," or "they're high
to-night," or "flying westwards now, I think." He
announced this very dramatically, but to the others sitting
there they seemed like the bits and ends of some crazy
geography.

"I say, just listen to the bloody mouses," but nobody
appeared to hear him.

Gwen had sat holding Mr. Frazer's hand, she felt she had
been holding some wild, fluttering bird, it was all tremble.
Emily's hand was on her husband's knee.

"Comfy, dear ?" Emily would say, and he grunted, "Yes."

Sometimes all three of them would talk very low, a sort
of mumble-jumble language which none understood.

"You comfortable, Mrs. Frazer ?" Gwen would say,
and Emily would reply,

"Yes, dear. Quite, thank you."

Mrs. Robinson had dozed off, but Mr. Robinson found it
very difficult to sleep at all, difficult to sit still, Automatically
his fingers went to the Philco, it all seemed very still to him,
who always had his ear to the staggering world outside.
Again he said, "Listen to the mouses," he was getting excited,

they seemed determined to let him go on enjoying the company of his own voice.

"Christy ! Can't you hear the mouses, ducksie ?"

"Sure you're both comfortable ?" Gwen said, and Mr. Frazer said, "Ah !" and then "Oh !" and Emily her usual "Yes, dear."

Gwen wondered about Richard. Wondered where he could be. He seemed to have been out years. She prayed he would be safe, prayed he would be back soon. Her mind was full of Richard. She could feel a weight on her shoulder, gradually the old man's head had come to rest there. The candle spluttered, it went out.

"Please light another candle," Gwen said.

"Merry hell, yes," the blue man said, paused, added, "that is, if I can find the stinking matches."

He was searching frantically for these, pawing the bench, feeling about on the mouldy floor, delving with violent hands into his pockets. "Oh hell !"

"Can't you find them ?" Gwen said.

The relief that this wireless was shut off had never left her. Against much pleading he had finally silenced it, first to a low trickle of music, as though hating to part with it, then finally out.

"Can't you find them ?"

"In a minute—yes."

But giving him no time she said, "Feel in the sailor's pocket, he's sure to have some."

"Yes, all right," the blue man said. He groped very carefully in trousers and coat pockets, the sailor did not stir, he was like a log, delicately the blue man felt, as though he half-expected to withdraw not matches, but a handful of mice. He said, "Got them."

Gwen was silent. Mr. Frazer was asleep, gently snoring, Emily too, had fallen asleep. The blue man struck a match, held it high, he surveyed the cellar and its occupants. "Damn," burning his finger, he struck another match. "Here we are."

"There's a whole packet of candles on the floor somewhere,'' Gwen said, not thinking of candles, her mind was full of Richard.

Mr. Robinson lit a fresh candle and stuck it in the tin on the wall. *"There ."*

"Thank you," Gwen said.

The blue man still stood there, surveying them, he burst out laughing, then sat down again. For the first time he saw that Mrs. Robinson had slipped to the floor.

"I say, ducks."

He shook her gently.

"I say, ducks, merry hell. You're on the floor," he was laughing again. He lifted her up, made her comfortable on the bench. "There, ducks," then with startled surprise, "I say, it's still asleep."

"Er ?"

"Dozy," he said, "what about a spot of coffee, ducks ?"

"I *am* thirsty, darling, let's."

She opened her eyes slowly, she looked down. "Poor podgy-wodgy," she said.

He got the thermos, he poured coffee into two blue bakelite cups. He got sandwiches out of a table napkin.

"I say, this is good," taking a mouthful, bending down, looking very closely at the child, he might give it a piece of mutton sandwich at any moment.

Fiercely in her ear, utterly confiding, "Christy ! I feel like a bloody little effing rat sitting here, ducksie, and those stinkers overhead."

"Oh, darling ! The way you talk. You can't leave me here, lovey-dovey."

"No ducks," kissing her, "I can't. That's right. Have some more coffee."

"That sailor——"

"John, bloody Johns or something," the blue man said, gulping coffee.

"He doesn't half sleep, anyway," Mrs. Robinson said.

"Had a sea of drink to-night, so's that piece there," finger pointing at Celia.

"Don't know how they can take the stuff."

"She's deado, too."

"Suppose so. Wonder what time it is," he was irritable again, he couldn't be still, not even eating mutton sandwiches, he couldn't even hear the mice, and they had been distracting.

"Merry hell, I wish the bastards would go."

"So do I, darling," ducksie said, she glanced down at the child, "poor old podgy-wodgy."

"Oh, bugger."

"*What*, darling, what ?"

"Oh, nothing."

"Let's go up," she said.

"It does stink, ducks, doesn't it ?"

"Let's go up, *darling*," she was making to get up, but he pushed her down again.

"Merry hell, you don't know what you're saying. You can't go yet."

"Oh, all right."

Softly in her ear, "Funny, isn't it. A mile up and you'd look like an insect."

She laughed, that could be funny, "and podgy-wodgy ?"

"Baby insect."

They both laughed softly, leaning against each other, their laughs embraced.

"You know it's just occurred to me that somebody's coming downstairs," he said.

"Who ?"

"That man, and that woman. He's cracked. I think. Intelligent rat. Got a huge picture there, calls it Daylight or something. She's ice. Oh yes, you can tell. Crack if she laughed. I offered to help them down, no bloody go, whole idea's balmy, anyhow. Yes, that's them coming down now. Now how the devil can they get the thing in here, it won't fit in at all. Suppose they'll get it in though."

"But they can't, darling ; where could they put it, any-how ?"

"Where could they ? That's what I say. More coffee, ducks ? No. All right, I'll have it then."

"He's the one who's always ill, or something," ducksie

said ; she was unconsciously rocking the child on her knee, which occasionally gave great sucks at nothing.

"Dunno ! Think that's all fuzz, *really*. Fact is he's been a traveller in vinegar, stinks of it," a fugitive laugh stole out, "funny how she sleeps through it," he said, taking the child's hand, feeling a petal softness against his hard, dry skin.

"Yes, isn't it. Oh, I do wish they'd go."

"They'll go," he said, definitely assuring, and then his fingers began to drum on the Philco, though he was quite unconscious of their doing so.

But Emily heard it and immediately woke up. She said, "Oh dear."

"Anything the matter ?" Gwen said.

Emily made no reply. She stood up.

"You can't go out, Mrs. Frazer," Gwen said, "good heavens. Please, do sit down. Where are you going ?"

"Out !" Emily said.

"But you can't," Gwen reached out a restraining hand, "please, you mustn't," thinking of Mr. Frazer, his head still on her shoulder, she was afraid to move, she loathed waking him up.

But Emily was moving away. Gwen eased the weight from her shoulders, she knew the old man would wake now.

"I'm going out," Emily announced.

"Er," Mr. Frazer said, "er," and then, "oh—you there, Emily, dear ?"

"I'm here," Emily said, "but I'm not staying here," she was moving towards the door.

"Oh dear," Mr. Frazer said, he staggered to his feet, he followed Gwen across the cellar, he doddered, he stumbled into Celia.

"Ow !"

The blue man laughed.

"Wait, Emily, wait, dear !" Mr. Frazer cried, "don't go. You can't go. A minute."

But Emily could not wait. There was no time. She was resolved. She was going out. She had been dozing but the blue man's drumming had woke her up. In her dozy mind the first thing she thought of was South America, the great forests there, her mind fumbled backwards through years, through clouds of fog, haze, backwards to when they were younger, Mr. Frazer and she, sleeping behind mosquito nets, when natives drummed in the forests. It was like that to her. She knew what drumming meant, danger. She must go out. A warning. She couldn't stay.

"Good Lord," the blue man exclaimed, "everybody's going out or something," seeing Emily going, Gwen behind her, Mr. Frazer doddering in her wake, "I say, ducks, every-body's going out."

The child woke up and cried.

"Wait," Gwen said, "come back, Mrs. Frazer," reaching for Emily's sleeve, grabbing it, "you mustn't, really," hold-ing on.

"Please, don't go, dear," Mr. Frazer said, "come back, Emily, is's dangerous, those people are still overhead, don't go, dear, please," mind doddering, feet doddering, what was all this about ?

He had been quietly dozing, and now everything seemed violent, urgent, people pushing each other about, a baby crying, something shouting, "Ow," it bewildered. What had happened ?   What was all this about ?

"Wait, Emily, dear," he cried, and against this the blue man shouted, "oh, I say there !   You can't do that.   Christy ! The raid's still on," but Emily was out, she had nicely manœuvred past Mr. Johns heaped.   She had got clear.

"Oh God," Gwen said, under her breath, Richard pressing hard in her mind, "oh God, I hope you're all right, Dick," then calling softly, calmly, "Come and sit down, Mr. Frazer," taking his hand, leading him back to his seat, thinking of his oldness, his doddery ways, Emily and he, they were like children, "Come now, sit down, she won't be long, she's gone up to get something, 'lying,' some something she forgot, there now," forcing him down on the bench, she sat by him, she took his hand again.

"Oh, God, Richard, I wish you were back, I wish you were back," the words singing in her mind, they were as fierce as flame. "Heavens," she shouted, "can't you keep that child quiet?" The candle flame grew bigger, sometimes it gave spasmodic upward leaps, the draught fanned, it would soon burn out.

"*Please!* Can't you keep it quiet?" she said, looking across at the Robinsons.

Mrs. Robinson looked at her but said nothing. She never spoke to Gwen, she knew her name was Jones, her blue man had told her about Mr. Jones being a bowler-hatted man.

Again Gwen said against child cries, "Do keep it quiet."

"Oh, I say, half a mo ducks," the blue man said, stopped suddenly, he thought, "she's got a mood." He watched podgy-wodgy jerked upwards, he heard her sing to it.

"Do de do de do de dah," then louder, "dad de dad de dad de de," determined to drown its cries, "luvum mumums luvum mumums, do de do de do."

"I say, you'll make her ill, ducks."

"Dum te dum te dum te tah," she sang, it was suddenly fierce, like battle cries. The child's face rose and fell against the candle light.

She felt the touch on her arm then.

"Shall I switch on, ducks?" he said, "it might stop her crying," and she said, wearily, "Oh, just as you think, *darling*," always she dragged this word, "oh, I wish we could go up. I wonder how long the beastly thing's going on?" her voice fell to whispers and he whispered back.

Mr. Frazer had a fit of coughing.

"Oh, dear! I do wish she hadn't gone out," he was getting up again, but Gwen made him sit down.

" She won't be long. I remember now, she went up to get something. Don't worry, Mr. Frazer, besides it'll be all over soon."

Anything to keep him quiet. She wished Richard were here. He *could* manage things.

"Will she be long, d'you think she'll be long, Mrs. Jones ? "

"No ! She'll be back any minute."

"But are you sure, Mrs. Jones ? You see—lately—I mean —well Emily——"

"Yes," Gwen said, and then was silent. She couldn't think of another word to say. All the words had been used, she went on holding his hand, she thought, "It can't go on very much longer, *very* much longer," making the words a cradle, rocking herself there, assuring, believing, " not very much longer, surely, he's *sure* to be back soon."

She sat very still, she held on to this thought. Mr. Frazer mumbled, he took Gwen back through years of his life, when Emily and he were young.

.   .   .   .   .   .

"Ten steps," Emily said, "I know there's ten steps," counting, as she went up, "one—two—three——" her mind was full of stairs. "Four—five—six——" as she went on, her black gloved hand pawing at damp wall, feeling the tang of night air on her cheeks, but she looked at nothing, neither sky, nor building's shape, there was no time. "Seven—eight —nine——" she would soon be on ground level, she felt the damp through her gloves. She was out. She could never have sat there, not after that low drumming. She was out and she had taken with her the drift of their words.

"It's dangerous. Don't go yet, Mrs. Frazer"—"wait a minute, Emily," which was the very thing she could not do. She had to go. She knew this. Though she liked Mrs. Jones as much as she liked Mr. Jones, she could not stay, and her soft Welsh words were nothing. She could not think of fifty years of loyalty doddering behind her. "Nine—ten," she said, stopped, she took a deep breath.

"I'm out," she said, "I'm out," and then she felt wooden floor beneath her.

Below Mrs. Frazer took Gwen right back to his boyhood, and she listened to him, but only because it could be distracting.

Emily had reached the foot of the stairs. Now she stopped again.

She was listening to something, she thought she heard shuffling sounds over her head. Like Mr. Robinson she thought of mice. In the darkness of hall, on the stairs, in all the rooms of this house, mice, there might be thousands of them, all nibbling. Holding on to the stair-rail, she started to go up, she was counting again. "one—two—three——" she knew the fifth was smashed. Passing it, you leaned close against the wall, she counted "four."

She mumbled. "I ought never to have gone down. I know now," thinking of Mr. Jones's thunderous "everybody down," of his direct authority, but the golden touch about him existed no longer.

"How dark it is," she was past the fifth stair. "I'm out, anyway, that cellar——" thinking of the music there, of Mr. Robinson. He was just like a notice being served on you, "herewith the first touch on to-morrow," still thinking of him as she counted "eight—nine," wondering how long his leave would last. She rested.

"There they are again, that Mr. Robinson was right all the time. The place is simply full of mice. 'Ten—eleven—twelve—thirteen' Oh ! " she shouted with sudden fright.

"It's all right," Lena said, "it's only me," a hand on her arm.

"Oh ! What's that ? " Emily said.

"Only me," Lena said.

"You."

"Yes, Mrs. Stevens."

"Oh—are you still here ? "

"Where are you going to ? " Lena said.

"Upstairs to my room," Emily said, endeavouring to force a way past, "I *must* get past," as though the older woman were deliberately barring her path, "let me go," she said, but Lena was not in her way, the path was clear, her hand did not touch Emily, she was free to go. "Let me go," Emily said.

"There ! " Lena said, she switched on the torch. They stared at each other.

"Yes, that's right. A label round their necks, 'Lost,' " Lena thought.

Emily saw the man sitting on the stairs, he was crouched close to the wall, his two hands pressed flat against his face.

"Oh, is that you, Mr. Stevens. Oh dear, you have those awful headaches, don't you? I heard about it. Mr. Jones told me. Dear, dear!" She bent down, was consoling, "you know, Mr. Stevens, you ought to take those Aspro's for your headaches, always Mr. Frazer and I take them. They are very good, *very* good. Whenever those people are over we take them. Are you going down to the cellar?"

"Yes, we're going down," Lena said.

"But you should hurry, you know. Oh, you should hurry. This evening when the horns went," she always referred to the sirens as horns, "I had an idea they might be over a long time. Mr. Frazer, too. He thought the same as I did. Oh, what's that?" she said, with a child's surprise.

"A picture," Lena said.

"Oh—fancy."

"I'm taking it downstairs," Clem said, he removed his hand, stared at Emily.

"He always takes it down below whenever there's a raid on," Lena said.

"You know, dear," Emily said, catching hold of Lena's arm, "you know, I—if I'd known you were taking this big picture downstairs—I used to like pictures when my eyes were good—if you had called, I mean if Mr. Stevens had shouted, I'm sure that Mr. Jones would have helped, he's very kind."

"He did," Lena said, "but he had to go out."

"Yes. I know that. Every time those people come over he has to go out. Warden."

"Yes. D'you want to get past?"

"Yes, yes, I must go up," Emily said.

"Careful, Mrs. Frazer," but Emily bumped into Mr. Stevens, she was apologetic.

"I used to love painting myself once, Mr. Stevens, when my husband and I were in South America. I often used to paint the sunsets."

"That was nice," Lena said.

"Yes, wasn't it. My word, it is big, isn't it. I suppose cellars are the best place for them, I suppose they are."

"That's right," Lena said, she was looking at the canvas, suddenly realized they had forgotten the cloth.

"We forgot the cloth."

"What ? " Emily said.

"Get the cloth, Lena," Clem said.

"I suppose if there was any other place you could take it, you'd take it there," Emily said, addressing the man on the stairs.

Nobody answered her. She went up past them, she began to hurry.

"I'll slip up now," Lena said, she gave a little laugh, "fancy my forgetting the covering cloth, after all these years," following behind Emily, she came up with her.

"Do come," Emily said ; she seemed suddenly distraught.

"Anything wrong ? "

"I couldn't stay down there. I had to come up. I couldn't rest. I don't believe Mr. Jones will do anything at all, oh dear."

" I *am* sorry," Lena said, wondering to what the old woman was referring, hardly expecting the flood of words that followed.

"I couldn't stay. I can't sleep any more, he knows it. And something has happened to Mr. Frazer, he does everything the wrong way round. I couldn't sit there any longer," she gripped Lena's hand, she began pulling frenziedly, "we can't sleep any more."

They went along the landing.

"Wait," Emily said.

"All right, I'll wait," Lena said, she watched the old woman go into her room. The light was switched on, and Emily appeared again, standing inside the door.

"It won't shut, it'll never shut any more."

"Soon be put right. Mr. Jones will see to that."

"No ! It'll never shut properly again. I know."

"Lena."

"All right, I'm coming," she called down to him, "coming now."

She looked at Emily. "I'll come back," she said, " I must go," she said.

When she reached the top of the stairs she turned and looked back. Then she went upstairs again and did not stop until she reached her room. She went straight to the kitchen and filled a glass of water.

"My mouth feels so dry, so dry," she said. She went down to Clem, saw Emily standing in the doorway but she did not speak to her.

"Coming now," she called.

They covered the canvas, and Lena made the fastenings secure.

"All right," she said, lifting, "are you ready ? "

He didn't say anything, just lifted his end. They started off.

CHAPTER VI

Low, shuffling sounds, like a sly, slinking river after the roar of seas.

Then silence.

"How quiet it's gone," Mrs. Robinson said, and he said, "Yes ! Hasn't it ? "

"I believe I will have another cup of coffee after all," ducksie said.

"Isn't any, ducks, I drank it."

"Beast ! "

"Just looks as though they were courting," the blue man said, looking across at Mr. Frazer, his head on Mrs. Jones's shoulder, her hand in his. She never let go this hand. He was dozing again.

"I wish the all-clear would go," ducksie said ; she let fall a glance at the child, gave a slight sigh. "Asleep," she said She thought, "but for how long." She looked up at Mr. Robinson. "How I hate all this beastly business," she said, "oh *darling*."

He kissed her. He said, "Won't be long now, ducks. But Christy you feel like a trussed fowl here and no mistake. When I think of it. Monday I'll be up there, in the bloody skies. I'll see myself sitting down here, squat, bloody rat, worm, I'll say, 'you stinking little rat of a man.' "

He declaimed like an actor, "Lording over the Lord, Monday."

"How that sailor sleeps," Mrs. Robinson said.

Celia still slept. They looked down at her, but she was nothing, she had become disembodied, she was part of the cellar, they smiled at each other, and the blue man said, "tart."

"Wonder where she came from. How did she get in here ? "

"Wonder ? " Mr. Robinson said. "I—wonder. Both drinking in that flat. Don't know how they can take the stuff myself, honest I don't. Listen a minute," he said, gripping her hand.

"Listen what, darling ? "

"Nothing. I just thought I heard it then," he said.

"I'll hate Monday," she said.

"D'you ever ask yourself where all this is going to end, where it's all leading to, you know, how it'll all end sort of thing. Do you, ducksie ? "

"Afraid I don't, dear. I just think—well I'm breathing, and that's something."

"Um ! "

"Could *you* hear those bloody mouses before, ducks ? " he asked.

"Mice ! Silly, darling. It's those people coming down with the picture. Now just fancy all that fuss about getting a picture into a cellar. I should have thought that it was better to get *yourself* in, never mind pictures."

"Suppose those sort of people *are* queer. This piece here seems to have known him once upon a time. Heard her saying something about having sat for him years back. Suppose he's crazy, but the woman looks after him like a good 'un. I suppose you'd call it—oh well—you can't find the right word. You're right though, ducks, it is them. Fancy me thinking it was mice.''

He shouted, ''Shut that stinking door. Who's there? Watch the bloody light,'' then softly in Mrs. Robinson's ears, ''I wish those bastards would go. We could go up out of this.''

The door was dragged back. He got up and went to see what the row was about.

''Oh!'' laughing, ''so you got down all right,'' looking straight at Lena, he saw Clem behind, but he ignored him.

''I can't see how you're going to get that thing in,'' he continued, ''it won't fit at all. But I told you that already. You could have got it under the stairs, you know. Plenty of room there.''

''He wants it in here,'' Lena said, staring in the blue man's face, ''it will go in. Would you help?''

''All right, then,'' he said, deferential, ''all right, but I told you,'' he grasped one end of the weight and began to carry it inward.

''Careful! Careful there.''

It was Clem.

''Nice to hear you say something,'' the blue man said; thought, ''Christy! Who wound him up? I suppose—I suppose it isn't funny to them, something drives them to do these things, queer crowd—all right, lift your end.''

He gave Mr. Johns a poke with his pointed shoe, he thought Mr. Johns had slept quite long enough.

''Here! Come on! Wake up there. Shift your carcass,'' he said, ''wake up.''

Mr. Johns broke wind, slowly he sat up.

''Bugger me,'' he said, and blinked at everybody.

''Come on, get out of the way,'' the blue man said, poking at Johns again.

Without a word the sailor staggered to his feet, moved back, promptly sat down again with his back to the wall.

''Can't you do anything, sitting there like a bloody owl?''

Mr. Johns went on blinking, he liked being an owl.

They finally got the canvas in, and now stood grouped

around it. The low ceiling prevented heads from being raised, they looked like a committee full of weighty decisions about the picture.

"Ow ! "

Everybody looked at everybody. It was so sudden that even the blue man jumped, the sound tore through the cellar.

"Get off my leg, will you ? " said Celia, now fully awakened from her sleep, landfall after the long voyage in seas. "Get off my leg."

"We can't just stand here like mummies," Mr. Robinson said, "can we ? " finally appealed to Mrs. Robinson, "now can we, ducks ? D'you think this will fit in anywhere ? "

"Doesn't look like it, darling, does it ? "

"It just doesn't. You're right, ducks," He turned to Lena, "D'you positively *have* to have the thing in here ? "

"Is it in your way ? " she said.

"I wonder sometimes whether these sort of people do realize there's a stinking bloody war on," musing.

"Hell no ! It's not in my way," he looked at them all, as if to say, "now is it ? "

"I think you might get it in there," Gwen said. She called out, "there."

She wanted to help, she felt sorry for Mrs. Stevens, ever since Richard had shouted at her outside their flat door. Sorry for her, but she could not fathom the man. He was mystery.

"I'm sure it would go over there," she called out again, "if you shifted those things out of the way. It would go behind the—anyway, there's no room anywhere else, I'm certain."

Celia stood up, she staggered about, her head felt heavy, it swung on her shoulders, she suddenly sent a shower of titters flying.

"Oh, Christ," she said, "*Oh*, Clem ! Here you are. You and your bloody masterpiece."

"You get out of the damned way," the blue man said, "you're just everybody's nuisance."

"Who're you shovin', who d'you think you are ? " Celia

said ; she laughed in his face. "Oh, Clem ! Lor ! You aren't half stuck-up, eh, don't know me now, do you ? Sat for you many a time, oh aye. Didn't half like me, you didn't. Stuck-up," she addressed the assembly. " He's been working on that for years, bloody years, but he never finishes anything, do you, Clem ? "

"Look out of the way," Mr. Robinson said, giving her another push.

"Nothing ever is," Lena said.

They dragged the weight further in.

The blue man looked at Mrs. Jones, "I say, couldn't you make this noisy child sit down," a direct appeal.

"There's a seat here," Gwen said, moving up.

Celia sat down. She hardly realized she was trembling, violently trembling.

Mr. Robinson dragged out the dustbins, the lids made loud, clanging noises.

"Oh, Clem ! Oh, Clem ! " Celia shouted across, "in amongst the muck after all."

"Are you cold ? " Gwen said ; she couldn't ignore this trembling, she could feel it like convulsions against her own body, "are you cold ? " gripping the young woman's arms, holding her tight, "why, you're shaking all over."

Celia opened her mouth, but nothing came out, she glared at Gwen.

"They're back ! Oh, God ! There they are ! They're back."

"Who ? What's the matter ? "

"I'm frightened," Celia said. "Oh God, I'm scared, I feel them coming."

She felt them again, the cosmic coldness creeping down on her.

"There ! Have a drink. Some hot coffee here," Gwen said, putting her arms round Celia. "I wish my husband would come back. This is dreadful."

"Well ! There it is at last, anyhow," the blue man said.

It was securely against the wall, and the dustbins were back in place.

"Thank you," Lena said. She took Clem's arm. "Come and sit down."

They sat by the Robinsons. She whispered to him, she gave him something to drink, she asked him if he wanted a sandwich, if he was comfortable, if his headache had gone now. She sat close. She didn't see anything in particular, not a thought stirred, she didn't feel a thing. She sat very still.

Celia screamed, and Gwen held her tight, saying, "There, there," and "THERE."

"Oh, Richard, I do wish you were here," the words made circles in her mind.

"Ssh !" the blue man said, "you'll wake it up."

He sat beside Mrs. Robinson, his knees drawn up, hands clasped round them. In a low voice he talked to ducksie.

"Won't be long, ducks. Soon be up now." He put an arm round her. "Funny, it's bloody funny. Monday I'll be up, I'll be looking at myself curled up here, scared rat. Monday I'll be high. Hell, how the place does stink, doesn't it, ducks. Wish I was up there, shooting those bastards down. You feel helpless like this," in a very low voice, "like this chap here, little mouse, you hate yourself. You know where you should be, ripping clouds up, getting after the swine. Oh, but you wouldn't understand, ducks, I mean how you feel when you're up, high up, oh higher than high."

"Oh, don't talk any more, *please*, darling," ducksie said.

Even Bolivia was better, the whole thing made her sick It was beastly. She hated him going Monday.

She didn't know that Mrs. Stevens had been staring at her husband all this time, did not know how he fascinated, she could not take her eyes off him, and was only aware of this when the woman said in a quiet voice, "When you are up on Monday, Mr. Robinson, I should shoot out the stars. I wonder why you've left them shining so long."

But the blue man did not hear, he had turned on his wireless. The music crept up, slow, stubbornly climbing. Bolivian rhythm strongly affected Mr. Johns, who quite unknown to

them had got back into his old position, he seemed to like
being heaped by the door, he began to sing.

> Oh—when I was a sailor, a bloody old sailor
> Sailing on the good old sea,
> Oh when I was a sailor, sailor, sailor, sailor,
> On the good old, bloody old, bloody old, good old sea.

his voice climbed with the music, then rose and fell as though
in rhythm with waves.

"There they are," Celia shouted, trying to break free from
Mrs. Jones, "there they are. I knew, I knew."

"Merry hell," the blue man shouted, "they're low again,
blast them, oh ducksie, ducksie ! " then louder, "get down,
everybody, quickly, quick, close to the wall," shouting louder
still, "close, close up to the wall. Hang on to me, ducks,"
hearing it coming down, down, shielding her, pressing her
flat, whilst Bolivia fought it out with down screaming sound.

"Jesus ! " Gwen said, "Richard," she cried in her mind.
"Oh, Richard, Richard."

Sounds deafened them, and they were heaped, Mrs. Robinson covering child, Gwen and Mr. Frazer and Celia wrapped
close, Clem and Lena pressed to the wall, pressed hard, like
the giant endeavour of bone to force a way through this,
and the door blown, and Mr. Johns flung into the air, the
reeking air.

The noise died away. Clem turned from the wall and
looked towards the door, suddenly shouted, "I must see this.
I must see this," let go Lena's hand, the warmth and pressure
and great trust that filled it, he jumped up shouting, "I must
see this. I must see this."

"Wait ! Wait ! " Lena said, "I'll come with you, wait,
I'm coming now."

Fugitively from a dark corner, "Are you all right, ducks,
are you—— ? "

"Let go," Clem shouted, "let go, I must see this," watching
the river of light flowing past, and then he saw Mr. Johns
lying just outside, lying there, and he looked at him for a

moment or two, and then he stepped over his great shuddering arse.

"Wait, wait ! I'm coming," Lena shouted. The child sucked horror home. Clem ran out.

CHAPTER VII

EVERY level of air hurling as he ran, and wherever he ran he saw that great shuddering sailor, dark against the river of light, against a reeling wall, looming up as from some great hole in the earth, the great shuddering sailor. He stopped dead, looked up, light was scattering light, a steeple careered crazily through space, under his feet a river in tumult, flowing wild. Great engines roaring past, and faces, faces, faces. He ran up some steps, he reached a roof, he leaned against the iron railings and he watched, he felt tremble under him, the city rocked with outrageous power. A life lived to see this. A great wall collapsing, a door hurling in the air like a demented sail, caught in a wind deluge, a falling girder. He could feel the pressure of the earth under him, he let go the railings and ran across the flat roof to the other side, he clung with one hand to an iron gate, it collapsed at a touch. And always the light sweeping past, as though blown by the great wind, a life lived to see this, a grey city rocking. Not what you felt, you couldn't even think, mind's doors closed up. It was what you saw. He stared entranced at the blazing sky. All that light, a sea, an ocean of light, from what vast reservoir had it flooded up, this drenching light, blazing red, and suddenly to his left a falling green, cataracts of light, red, and yellow and green, this riot of colour shouted at you.

"God ! " he said, "it's magnificent, it's——"

He turned and ran across the roof again, went down the iron ladder, took stone steps at a leap, he ran on through the streets, he felt the wind behind, the pressure under flying feet. From what dark hole the wind, by what touch the light. He turned a corner and knocked a man down, he did not

wait, he ran on. Somewhere there was a high place, higher
than that roof, something high up from pressure and from
frenzied wind, a calm oasis, a place to stand, to watch this.
The darkness gone, the lurk and the leer that it could hold.
He saw a whole forest of writhing snakes, silver under the
light.

"You goddam fool. Where you running to ? "

He didn't hear, didn't feel, he only saw. He ran on. He
was drenched to the skin.

He came to a great building, he watched it sway. Higher
than any building he had ever seen. He went through a gate,
he groped his way until he found what he wanted, the iron
staircase that spiralled to roof-top. He began to ascend.
Every few steps he stopped to look down, a blackness below.
He felt the mass of iron throb as he climbed. Life had come
to iron, steel, to stone. He went on, and now he did not look
back any more. He kept a firm grip on the rail, he looked
skywards at the light. Far below in the street a grinding of
brakes, hissing noises, but always the light overhead, reeling,
bright colours, like an overflow from revelries. He reached
the top, breathing heavily, he was on the roof. Wood and
stone and steel alive with wrecking power. Roads opened,
streets collapsed, hollow sounds where once old giants had
stood, great gaps, fissures, rivers in tumult, showering glass,
old giants flat. He looked down from the heights. An orgy
of movement, in one direction, moving under the light. An
ocean of floating trash.

A battering sound below, something white threshing in the
black moving sea. He could see this, he went on watching it.
Suddenly he walked off the roof, he began to descend. Above
the uproar he heard these sounds distinct, something alive,
battering against stone, he hurried down, he reached the
ground, and started to run in the direction from which the
sounds came. A series of clattering sounds and he was
close up to the white threshing thing. He reached out his
hand, something seemed to explode under it. A mad beast
threshing, he knew it was a beast, he felt electric waves running across its back. He grabbed at the head, he caught hold

on a leather, he was jerked into the air, the beast dragged him after it, they were in the street, they were in the middle of this down-rushing sea. Its forelegs rose up, threshed empty air, it plunged wildly, it careered on down the street. And then against the light he saw it real. A big white stallion loose, a maddened animal, he held on, he could not let go his hold on this. He felt himself dragged, he did not resist, he let it pull him along. A smell came to his nostrils, he looked ahead, and then he pulled hard on the leathers. The maddened beast was dragging him towards a fire, he got the pungent smell strong in his nostrils. Gripping the leathers with both hands he pulled with all his strength. It was like pulling against tides, the enormous strength terrified him, he felt humbled by this plunging beast. Beads of sweat rose on his forehead, he again pulled. The horse reared up, he lost his footing, he felt himself dragged, he was now one with all this rushing ocean. It reached a cross-roads and began to gallop, but always he held on, grimly, as though all his life had been a single movement towards this, to hold fast with a hoofed creature, demented in a rocking city. His body hung heavily, the world was upside down as he looked, the world itself was shaking under the beast's thunder.

Then of a sudden it stopped. For a moment he hardly realized it. He drew himself up, he refused to believe. But it was still, as though calmness had flowed over them. He looked into the big eyes, he delighted in their liquid light. Fear had gone. He put his hand on its back, he felt sweat there, then he patted its neck. Its head was over his shoulder, and he was delighting in the calm that flowed from this once plunging horse. Its flesh shuddered gently under his touch, he could feel the quiver under the nostrils. He leaned against it, he knew it was calm, it was safe. He picked up the leathers, walked slowly down the shattered street ; it followed after him, huge, shy, and shambling. How obediently it followed him.

If you walked far enough you came to something green, older than steel or stone, where this beast belonged. He kept on patting its neck, he suddenly loved this beast, a giant trust

lay between them, first demented and now calm, it would go
where he went. He never once looked back, he walked on,
horse shambled after him.

.   .   .   .   .   .

"Listen," Gwen said, and they listened.

"Yes, it is," Gwen shouted excitedly, "thank God it's all
over."

She kept looking at Mrs. Stevens, who sat with her hands
gripping the bench. Her head low on her breast, and all this
time she had not moved.

"Is it really," Celia said, "is it really ? "

"Yes, it's just gone," Gwen said, who thought of Richard
coming home.

When the others had gone she would take Mr. Frazer up.

"Come on, ducks," the blue man said, "it's all over.
Let's get up."

He helped her up, he took the child from her, and immediately it was awake, and crying again. "Oh damn ! All
O.K., ducks.   Get the other things, will you ? "

"Your *set*, darling," she said, in a kind of half-frightened
whisper.

"Yes, I can manage that," he said, he picked up the wireless,
and they went slowly out.

Mr. Johns had not moved. The party stopped. Mr.
Robinson put down his Philco, he leaned over the sailor.
"By God, you could sleep through anything," he said,
then he picked up his set and they went out, climbed stone
steps with great effort, and were gone, their footsteps died
away.

"Have you far to go ? " Gwen said, she had a restraining
hand on Celia, as though for some reason she did not wish
her to leave. "How far ? Would you like a nice hot cup
of tea if I make it ? "

"No ta," Celia said, her head was much lighter. "I've
not far to go. I know my way all right. Thank you just the
same. Good-bye," and she walked to the entrance.

She, too, stopped where Mr. Johns lay, she bent over him, she thought of ice, of plenty of *stuff*, the green room.   How clumsy and awkward he was really, a great baby.

"Are you going to sleep for ever ? " she said, looking into his face, at the long nose, the half-open mouth, the thick, lost lips. "Are you—my God ! Oh——" she said.

She went back to Gwen, who was helping Mr. Frazer to his feet.

"He'll never reach Plaistow," she said, and, "you ought to get the warden quick."   Then she went out.

Gwen did not move.   She stood Mr. Frazer on his feet, he didn't appear to understand anything she said ; she kept looking over at Mrs. Stevens.

"A minute," she said, sitting the old man down again. She went to the woman, she sat down, she found her softly crying.

"Oh, I am sorry," she said, "I'm so sorry——"

Lena looked up.   "It's nothing.   I must have been dreaming.   I'm all right."   She flicked fingers across her face.

"Are you sure ?   Your husband, he'll be all right.   He'll come back."

"Yes, he'll come back.   I know that.   I've always known it.   It wasn't that, it was something else."

"What, dear ? " Gwen said, for the first time she had used the word "dear."

"Nothing !   How relieved you'll be when Mr. Jones gets back."

"I believe that's him coming now," Gwen said, hearing steps down the street, she could not fail to recognize them.

Lena did not hear.   She was back twenty years, back in bright days.

"Gwe—n," Richard called, "Gwe—n."

She saw him in the doorway.   "Darling !   At last !   Oh, I'm glad you're safe," running forward to embrace him, and then she stopped.

There was Mr. Johns, like a great dividing sea.

"Oh, darling," she said.

"All right, dear," Richard said, out of a blackened mouth,

looking at her from red-rimmed eyes, "everything's O.K., dear."

"It's Mr. Johns," Gwen said.

"Mr. Who ? "

"The sailor, dear," she said, looking at the man on the floor.

"Oh ! I see," Richard said, "didn't know what you meant at first, God, I'm so glad you're all right, dear," reaching across the dividing sea, touching her hand, getting the warmth there, then letting it go, he was kneeling down. He was looking closely at the sailor's face, ashen now, the closed eyes and heavy lids, the utter trust in the hands' gestures, he felt his mouth.

"O Lord ! "

He opened his vest, his shirt.

"Poor chap," he said, and stood up.

Still dividing sea, he would not cross this man, not even to get her warmth.

Gwen seemed rooted where she stood.

"Everybody else up, dear ? " he said.

"Yes, just Mr. Frazer and Mrs. Stevens."

"Oh ! Isn't he there then ? "

"He ran out."

"Ran out. What on earth for ? "

She shook her head. "Oh, I don't know. Why talk ? "

" Who's that ? Somebody banged that door," Richard said.

"I don't know, dear."

It was Celia. She had Clem's picture under her arms, she had got it from its hiding-place under the stairs. She was going off down the street. She knew the way to go, she always did.

Richard took a whistle from his pocket and gave a blow on it. "Half a sec., dear," he said ; he got his hands under the sailor's shoulders, he dragged him clear from the entrance.

"There ! Poor old sailor," he said.

"Oh, darling," she said, flinging herself into his arms. They clung to each other.

The fresh candle was burning fast in the holder, a light wind fanning it, it stood directly over Lena's head.

She sat quite still. She was like floor, like wall, stone to this stone. She was waiting for Clem. She knew he would come back. He would never leave her, never. He was safe, he was coming back to her, she felt this. She must wait. And then they would climb again, back to their shell, where hollowness was, to the pain in the chest and the pills, and thoughts of Flo, and all that Essex green. To the cold room, and the Arctic touch.

They would go up together.

She raised her head, hearing loud voices. Two men were standing in the doorway, one, whose voice she recognized, was looking directly at her.

"It's all over, you know," Richard said ; he wondered if she knew.

"Is it ? " Lena said, wondering what was over. What was he talking about ? She turned round, she watched them lift up the sailor, they went away with him.

"And you go right up now, darling," Richard called to Gwen, "and remember I want that tea really hot, *boiling*. All right, Harry," he said, with lowered voice. " Can you manage ? "

"Yes, I can manage. I put this poor devil in here only a few hours ago. Said he'd been on the ice."

"Ice," Richard said, "I wondered where he came from. Drank a lot."

"I should say so," the other said ; he looked down at Mr. Johns. "Don't think he ever felt anything."

"He was just unlucky," Richard said. "They live hard, don't they ? "

"Aye ! They do that."

The words floated into Lena's ears. She knew what it meant.

"Poor shouter," she said, "poor shouter."

She could hear them climbing the steps, they died away into street sounds. Clem came in. He was standing there right in front of her, and she did not realize it.   But she knew his touch and looked up.

"Oh ! " she was on her feet, holding him fiercely to her.

"Clem," she said, "oh, Clem. Why did you run out ? "

"I wanted to see it," he said.

"To see what ? "

"Everything."

He was panting with exertion.   "I freed it," he said.

"Freed it ? "

"Yes, the horse.   I left it in a field."

"A horse.   You—why, you're shaking all over," she said.

"We had better go up now," he said.

"Sit down, rest a while, you've no breath left," forcing him down.

"No, no, let's go up now," he said.   "Help me to get the canvas out."

He was suddenly staring towards the door.

"What is it ? " she said.

He didn't answer, he only saw the sailor lying there again.

"Nothing."

"That sailor," she said, "he——" and then she was thinking of stairs, counting them in her brain.

"Sailor ? "

"Yes.   Are you ready now ? "

"I'm ready now," she said.

THE END

FROM

ANDRE DEUTSCH

105-106 Great Russell Street
London WC1 Tel: 01-580 2746 Fax: 631 8253

FOR REVIEW

NO DIRECTIONS

James Hanley

Introduction by Henry Miller

£5.99 (paperback)

**Publication
Date**   August 9 1990

It is requested that no review should appear before publication
date. For further information please contact

The Publicity Department

André Deutsch 105-106 Great Russell Street London WC1